Short Sweetz 2

# Bonjour Chérie

Robin Martin

Published by Bennett Lane Press 2020



www.robinmartinthomas.com



Disclaimer
Every effort has been made to ensure that this book is free from error or omissions. Information provided is of general nature only and should not be considered legal or financial advice. The intent is to offer a variety of information to the reader. However, the author, publisher, editor or their agents or representatives shall not accept responsibility for any loss or inconvenience caused to a person or organisation relying on this information.

Book cover design and formatting services by Self-PublishingLab.com

ISBN:
9780648925804 (pbk)
9780648925811 (e-bk)

*To the 3 Rs:* Rob, Ruth, and Richard—*my little family,
who are my biggest cheer squad!*

# Chapter One

I was going to Paris. That was a definite. But with $87.50 in my savings account, there was a tiny question mark over when. Optimism, however, was my middle name. I had visualised it, and completed my dream board with pictures of Le Tour Eiffel, Champs Elysée and Toulouse Lautrec reproductions. I had a bottle of Chanel Number Five perfume from last Christmas that I was still eking out. I was even taking French evening classes. Really, except for the fine print, I was there.

Added to my wish list was my French teacher, Monsieur André LeBlanc, charming, good looking and cultured. He had an accent that made you think of midnight strolls under the moonlight, long, lingering looks over a glass of red wine, and slow dancing to soft music in smoky, intimate Parisian nightclubs. What he was doing in this small Queensland town, I couldn't imagine. Unless it was to meet me. There you go, the law of attraction. I wished it, thought it and, voilà, Andrè Le Blanc came to Clearwater Creek to teach French. Don't tell me the power of positive thinking doesn't work.

André's silky, dark hair bushed his collar, and his liquid brown eyes were intense and mesmerising. He moved with the grace of a ballet dancer. From the moment we met, I knew we made a connection.

There was the slight problem that Andre hadn't yet realised the powerful attraction between us. Perhaps he was shy. After all, we had only had three French lessons. It would take time for him to acknowledge what was so obvious to me, we were meant for each other.

It was our fourth lesson and we were learning how to introduce and describe ourselves. 'Je m'appelle Mademoiselle Elizabeth Jenkins,' I said to Mrs Ingham.

I went on to describe my long auburn hair and green eyes.

'Très bien, Mademoiselle Jenkins.' André beamed at me. I flatter myself my accent was very good. I twinkled a modest smile back at him as Mrs Ingham began a complicated sentence that told him she had blue eyes and blonde hair.

At that point, the door opened, and a guy came in. 'Is this Introductory French?'

André looked up. 'Yes, it is.' Three short words in that hot French accent.

'Sweet. I'm one of your students, Zach Mills.' He slid into the class with a confidence bordering on arrogance.

Tight jeans and a tighter black tee shirt. He flashed me a smile. He was clearly one hundred per cent Aussie. Forget it.

André frowned. 'The class has already commenced, depuis…since three weeks.'

'No worries, mate. I cleared it with the office. I'm good to go.'

'You may have to catch up…' André gave him a dubious look.

'I'm sure some of the students here—' He looked at me meaningfully, '—will be happy to help me.'

André gave a Gallic shrug and said, 'Please join us, Monsieur Mills.'

He sat next to me. I ignored him and turned to look at André, who had moved back to the front of the class. We went through the months of the year and the seasons and then, sadly, class was over for another week.

I was about to ask André about homework, when Mr Confident turned to me and said, 'Well, babe, what's your name?'

I gave him an impersonal look. He might as well know from the beginning I wasn't interested. 'Elizabeth Jenkins.'

He gave me a lazy smile, 'Good to meet you, Liz. You want to grab a coffee or something? It seems I have a few things to catch up on. I'd love some help.'

'It's Elizabeth,' I corrected him. I hated when people automatically changed my name. My friends called me 'Beth', but he was not a friend. 'I'm sorry, I don't have the time.' I got up from my seat and moved away from him. Surprise was etched on his face What? Didn't he think any female could turn him down, even for a cup of coffee?

André, putting his notes in his brown leather attaché case, looked up and smiled as I reached his desk. 'Yes, Mademoiselle Jenkins?'

'Beth,' I said and gave him a wide smile. I had mentioned this before, but perhaps he forgot. 'I was wondering if you had any homework.' It came out sounding breathy and shy.

'You could have a look at the links I gave you for the 'net. There are a couple of conversation exercises there.'

'Oh yes, of course, thanks for reminding me. I'll do that,' I gushed, sounding exactly like a thirteen-year-old with her first crush. Where was that confident chick who handled men as easily as a pizza chef tossing dough in the air and catching it with casual expertise?

As I tried to think of something else to say, he gave me a nod and disappeared out the door. With an inward sigh, I turned to leave. Obviously, he was too reserved to make the next move. It must be that teacher-student thing. I'd have to think of something by next week. It was only a ten-week course and we were nearly halfway through. If only he had asked me for coffee instead of that new guy.

As if he'd read my thoughts, Zach Mills stood, folded his arms and leaned against the wall. The mocking smile he shot my way told me he had heard my bumbling attempt to engage our French teacher in conversation.

Raising my chin, I swept out the door as if he didn't exist. But I couldn't avoid hearing his whispered comment as I passed him. 'Way to go, *Beth*.'

How could you dislike a person in such a short period of time? I'd make sure I sat as far away from him as possible next week.

The parking lot behind the institute was nearly deserted by the time I reached my battered little Datsun. I really needed a new car, but my job at the local IGA wouldn't quite cover that, especially if I was planning to go to France in the near future. I turned the key to start the engine and it gave an arthritic cough. I wasn't worried. It often needed a bit of encouragement to get going. I tried it again. *Splutter, splutter.* And again. And again. The battery light came on.

*Fantastic. Great. Way to go, girl.* Why couldn't this happen in the driveway at home? Or at least in daylight? Both Mum and Dad were away for a few weeks on holiday at the coast. I could call the RACQ, if I was still a member.

But my membership had lapsed three months ago, and I hadn't renewed it because…I was saving for France.

Frustrated, I rested my forehead on the steering wheel. Just as I realised I would have to call a cab to get home and wait until morning to deal with this, I heard a tap on the windscreen. I jerked upright, hoping like crazy that I'd locked my car door.

Dark eyes peered through the glass. *Zach.* Of course, it would have to be him. My day was just getting better and better. I rolled the window down.

'You okay?' He asked.

I wished I could tell him to get lost, but considering my situation, that wouldn't be wise. 'I think my battery's flat.' I tried to start the car again, but it gave a tiny burp like a baby and went silent.

'Don't try it anymore, you'll flood the engine,' he said, stating the obvious. I'm not totally stupid where cars are concerned, just broke.

He looked at me, hesitating for a moment, then said, 'I've got some jumper leads at home. I could go back and get them?'

I considered this. I didn't really want to accept help from this guy, who would no doubt use it to his advantage. Even the way he was standing told me that. His hands were on his hips, and he was probably secretly (or not so secretly) smirking at me, especially since I'd turned down his offer of coffee and now had to accept help from him. Calling an Uber would cost twenty dollars minimum, not to mention having to come back tomorrow and pay for a new battery. I considered my bank account. Low. I considered my pride. High.

'No thanks. I'll be fine.'

'Really? What are you going to do?'

As if that was any of his business. 'I'll just make a few calls. Thanks for the offer,' I said, trying to be polite, but dismissive.

He stood there looking down at me, dark-brown hair just skimming his eyes and a look on his face that said he didn't quite believe me. Of course, with his muscles and tan, he was your typical alpha male who probably put cars together in his backyard, watched the footy and drank beer. Not that there was anything wrong with that, for some people. But I was into cultured guys who listened to classical music, didn't mind watching ballet (or, at the very least, figure skating) and knew a thing or two about wine. Someone like…well, André. But André wasn't here and Zach was. And I wished he would stop staring at me like that and go away.

'Please, don't let me keep you,' I said, hoping he would get the hint.

'So, who are you going to call?' He was persistent.

I've always found it hard to lie, even when I really, really wanted to, like now. 'A friend,' I said vaguely. Well, an Uber driver could be a friend, couldn't he? Especially if he picked you up when you were in an awkward situation.

'I don't feel right leaving you like this. It's getting late and this isn't the safest area at night. So, go ahead and make your call and when I know someone is on the way, I'll leave. Okay?'

I so wished I could start my car and drive away leaving him standing open mouthed. But there was no way that was going to happen, at least not tonight. He looked like he had no intention of moving.

'I was going to call an Uber and come back in the morning.'

'So, you're not in the RACQ?'

'Isn't that obvious?' I snapped.

He sighed then said, 'Why don't you swallow your pride and let me help you? You can come with me while I get the jumper leads and then we'll head back here and get your car going.'

'I'll just stay here in the car until you come back. I'll lock the doors. I'll be fine,' I said for about the tenth time. I wasn't going anywhere with Zach Mills.

He shook his head and put his hands up in the air, 'I think you've already made it clear you're not interested in me and I'm not so desperate that I'd ask a girl out twice after she said no the first time. If you want to stay here, fine. I get it, you don't know me. But if my sister was stuck somewhere, I'd like to think someone would help her. I'll be back as soon as I can.'

I felt my face go warm with embarrassment. He was only trying to help, and maybe I was being hard on him. And, it was getting cold. With the engine not starting, I couldn't even turn on the heater. I climbed out of the car with as much dignity as I could muster. 'Okay, I'll come with you.'

'Your choice.' He stepped back and jerked his head, 'Ute's over there.' Then he walked away, leaving me to follow.

A black ute, of course. The only surprise I felt was that it didn't have cow hide seat covers or a sticker on the back saying 'Back off or else'. I climbed in on the passenger side, thankful he didn't feel the need to help me in or anything. I fumbled with the seat belt, which seemed to be caught in the door.

Muttering something under his breath, he leaned over from the driver's seat and opened the door, freeing the belt. I felt the warmth of his body and the scent of spicy aftershave (for sure it wouldn't be cologne) and a tremor of *something* went through me. His face was just centimetres from mine. I noticed the long lashes, chiselled cheekbones and strong chin that didn't seem to suit his macho personality. His eyes caught mine, and I swear he changed colour. But it must have been irritation and certainly not any attraction, because he jerked away from me, tossing the seat belt in my lap.

'Buckle up,' he said, as he started the engine, which unlike my little Datsun, roared to life.

I shrank into my corner as far as I could and looked straight ahead.

# Chapter Two

We kept up an icy silence that was almost more uncomfortable than talking. Zach had obviously decided he didn't like me, and the feeling was definitely mutual. It may have cost me my savings and even more on my credit card balance to have sorted this out on my own, yet that seemed a better option at the moment. Not that he had given me much choice.

I snuck a sideways look at him. His large hands gripped the steering wheel and he was staring straight ahead as if I weren't beside him. Suited me.

Now if this was André, we could talk about France. I would be happy to tell him about my dream of going there one day. We might even speak a little French together. Not that I knew much, but I would improve, especially with André's tuition. I immersed myself in daydreams (though I preferred to think of it as visualising) about the two of us walking hand in hand down a Paris street, his beautiful brown eyes looking into mine as he lifted my hand to his lips to kiss it when…*bump, clatter, clatter, clatter.*

'Damn,' said the very Australian voice beside me, jerking me from my thoughts.

'What happened?' I looked around at the dark shapes of trees on the side of the road. I hadn't paid much attention to where we were going, but I had a vague idea we were just north of the town, in the area where there were acreage properties and small farms.

Zach pulled the truck over to the side of the road and stopped. 'Flat tyre. Must have run over something on the road.' He opened the door and got out. Sighing, I slid out my side and went to have a look. The back, right tyre had been punctured and the truck was leaning to the side in the most depressing way. No way were we going anywhere until it was fixed. This night just kept getting better and better.

Zach had already swung into action, hauling out the spare tyre from the back as easily as if it were a donut. As he reached back in to grab the jack, he said, 'Can you get the torch from the glove box? I'm going to need you to shine it down here while I change the tyre. It's pitch-black and I won't be able to see a thing.'

As I crunched along the gravel shoulder to the cab of the ute, I winced. Heels, especially these ones, weren't the best choice for changing a tyre. Not that it looked like I was going to have to do much, as Zach was already loosening the bolts on the wheel and probably wouldn't have needed me at all, if it hadn't been so dark. I got the torch and wobbled back on the uneven ground, then my foot overturned just as I reached the back of the truck.

'Ow,' the small exclamation escaped before I could stop it.

Zach looked up, his eyes travelling from my faux alligator heels, to the skinny jeans, to the white top with lace edging and finally to my shoulder length auburn hair. It was too dark to read his expression, but there was no mistaking his disdainful tone when he said, 'You should take those shoes off before you do some serious damage. Why women torture their feet with shoes like that, I'll never know.'

'I wasn't exactly planning on being out in the bush helping change a flat tyre when I dressed tonight,' I snapped.

'No, you weren't, were you?' His white teeth shone in the darkness in a sudden grin. No doubt he was thinking I'd dressed to impress Monsieur André. He would be right, but I didn't like him knowing it.

Deciding to ignore that last remark, I switched the torch on. 'Let's just get on with changing this tyre, so we can get out of here,' I said.

'Too right, my thoughts exactly. Can you shine that torch on the tyre and not my face?'

We were getting on like a house on fire, weren't we?

However, he was quick. In less than five minutes, he had the old tyre off and the new one on. Flinging the old tyre in the back of the ute, he wiped his hands down the legs of his jeans. My eyes jerked back to his face. I didn't care how snugly those jeans fit his lean hips.

Maybe looking at him was a mistake altogether because his eyes locked with mine and he took a step closer to me. I wondered for one crazy moment what it would be like to kiss him. Then, a beam of headlights washed over us as a car whizzed past on the road. I took a step back and wobbled again as my right heel sank into the gravel, and I came back to my senses.

Zach put out a hand to steady me. 'You really ought to take those off. There's no one out here to impress, unless, of course, it's me.' There was that irritating grin again.

I jerked my arm away. 'Dream on.' I walked back to my side of the truck.

As we both got in, Zach said, 'Oh, I'm not the one who's dreaming, babe.' And before I could think of a reply, he started the engine and the truck roared to life.

It was obvious to me that while maybe four out of five girls might have liked Zach Mills, I was number five. He was arrogant and had an uncanny way of saying things that were guaranteed to annoy me. I couldn't wait until this night was over and I would never have to talk to him again, even in French class. Except, a small, inner voice said, he is helping you. Okay, I would be civil. That was it.

Thankfully, it wasn't long before he pulled into a gravel driveway that wound through the trees. We stopped in front of a low set brick house with a large shed beside it. Zach said. 'I'll be back in a moment. No need for you to get out.'

As Zach disappeared into the shed, I looked around with faint interest. Aside from an outside light, the house itself was in darkness. Did that mean he lived alone? Not that I cared. From what I could see, the place looked well-kept and tidy, if functional. I wondered what he did. Perhaps he was a tradie or a mechanic or…well, something physical and something outdoorsy, I was thinking.

I leaned back against the headrest and closed my eyes for a few minutes. It had been a long day and I was starting to feel tired. I couldn't wait until my little car started again and I was on my way home. Then, I realised there was another reason I really needed to get home. I needed to go to the bathroom. Surely, I could wait? No, I really couldn't. Now I would have to ask Zach if I could use the bathroom. *Great.*

I opened the door, slid out of the ute and headed for the shed. Then, I heard the click of claws on gravel and something the size of a small pony came bounding towards me. Deep chested barks exploded in the night air. Screaming, I fended off the two enormous paws that tried to attach themselves to my shoulders.

Zach was out of the shed like a flash. 'Down, Dave,' he called. *Dave*, my befuddled brain thought, whoever heard of a monster called *Dave*? A slobbery tongue licked the side of my face before I felt Zach pull him off me. 'Sit, Dave, behave yourself,' Zach said. The enormous creature sat beside him, tail wagging, but looking at me as if it were ready for another full-scale attack.

'Don't worry, he won't hurt you. He was just being friendly, weren't you, mate?' In answer, the giant's tail whisked even more frantically. 'You okay?' Zach looked at me.

'I guess.' I eyed Dave, waiting to see what he would do next.

'I thought you were going to stay in the truck?'

That reminded me why I had gotten out in the first place. The reason now seemed even more urgent than before.

'Umm…' I was so glad he couldn't see my cheeks redden in this light. "Well, I need to use your bathroom,' I said, trying to sound casual.

'No worries,' Zach said. 'Just follow me.' He led the way around the back of the house, where a light was on in the kitchen. I was glad to see that Dave, who had enthusiastically followed us, was left outside. Zach opened the door for me and said, 'Just down the hall to your right.'

My eyes flitted curiously around as I took in a neat, wood panelled kitchen that didn't have much in the way of decoration. However, I did notice a wine rack on the bench top. That surprised me. I could have sworn he was more the beer drinking type. Most likely the wine belonged to his folks.

I reached the small, clean bathroom with relief. As I washed my hands, I looked in the mirror and noticed my mascara had smudged, giving me large panda eyes. *Great,* I thought. Another thing for Zach Mills to find amusing. I washed my face as well as I could and decided not to reapply any make up. I wasn't out to impress anyone, that's for sure.

Zach was leaning against the kitchen sink, sipping a glass of water when I returned. 'You want a cold drink or…a coffee or anything?' I saw a twinkle in his eye as he said coffee. No doubt he was remembering a few hours ago when I'd turned down his offer of coffee. Didn't think he'd forget that in a hurry.

'I'm good,' I said. 'I probably should get back to my car. I wouldn't want anyone to…'

'Steal it? Sure. We'll get going.' He put the glass down.

Thinking about who would even bother with my battered little car, my face broke into a grin. 'Well, that would be optimistic thinking, wouldn't it? The insurance is probably worth more than the car.'

He laughed. 'Yeah, but then I'd have to drive you home and you wouldn't want that, would you?'

Without meaning to, I looked at him and there must have been something in my expression, because suddenly the teasing glint in his eyes was replaced by something else. For the second time that night I wondered what it would be like to kiss him. I took a small step towards him and our eyes locked. What can I say? We shared a moment.

Dave, waiting for us outside the kitchen door, gave a deep impatient bark. Whatever it was between us disappeared. I didn't know if I was relieved or disappointed. I moved towards the door. 'We'd better go.'

Zach must have felt the same way because he was at the door before me, opening it, 'Yeah, sure. Down, Dave, and, for God's sake, shut up.'

We were back in the ute and heading towards town before I felt more myself. Don't know what happened in the kitchen, but I was definitely over it. Perhaps it was just because I hadn't had a boyfriend in over a year. And since André Le Blanc had arrived in town, I hadn't wanted one, I reminded myself.

But at least the atmosphere between Zach and me was less frigid than it had been coming here. I could just about speak to him normally. 'So, why *Dave?*' I asked.

'You mean the name?'

'It's a bit unusual for a dog.'

'It's from David and Goliath.'

'What?'

'You know, the Bible story where the small guy, David, defeats the giant, Goliath, against all the odds.'

'Sure. But the giant was Goliath not David, so why didn't you call him Goliath?…Oh, I get it.' I shook my head, smiling. 'Aussie humour.'

'Yeah, it's like why we might call a big guy "Tiny", or a redhead "Bluey".'

'Clever.'

'I thought so.'

We drove along in almost amicable silence for a while. Then Zach said, 'So, Beth, what's your interest in French, other than Mr André?'

My back stiffened. I was quickly in the Antarctic zone again. 'I happen to have an interest in French culture, nothing to do with the instructor.'

He chuckled then said, 'Okay.'

How did he do it? How did he make me so angry with so few words? 'I'm going to France,' I shot back at him.

'When?'

'When I have saved enough. Not that it's any of your business.'

'None at all. Just asking.'

I sensed, rather than saw (no way was I looking at him), his grin in the darkness.

What was I thinking to even imagine for a nanosecond any smallI attraction between us earlier? With relief, I realised we had pulled into the parking lot where my small car stood in lonely isolation.

Zach was out and had the bonnet of both vehicles up and the leads attached almost before I had time to get myself behind the wheel of my car. Perhaps he was just as anxious to get rid of me as I was him.

'Start her up,' he said. My little car spluttered into life. I almost kissed the steering wheel.

After he'd detached the leads and put the bonnets down on both vehicles, he came over to me. I rolled the window down reluctantly.

'Do you want me to follow you back to make sure everything is ok?' he asked.

*Hell, no.* 'I'll be fine. Thanks for your help,' I said, remembering my manners.

'No worries. See you in French class, *chérie*.' And with a cheeky smile, he returned to his ute.

# Chapter Three

'**M**onsieur LeBlanc…André, how lovely to see you.' I beamed at him from the register as if he were a long-lost friend I hadn't seen in years, instead of four days ago. I pushed through his items—seedless green grapes (the expensive ones), brie cheese (of course) and rice crackers (99.9% fat free). I imagined myself sharing this with him over a mature bottle of red.

'How are you, Beth?' He remembered to use my first name. At last we were getting somewhere.

'Oh, just fine. I checked on those websites you gave me and I've been practising away,' I babbled.

'Good, good.' He stood there waiting patiently. What for? Perhaps he wanted to ask me out for a drink but was too shy to ask. I had nothing planned tonight. I could easily go. I mentally scanned the items in my closet, wondering what I should wear.

'Beth?' He spoke hesitatingly.

'Yes,' I answered, trying to look encouraging.

'How much do I owe?'

Flustered, I looked at the cash register. 'Twelve dollars sixty-five, please.'

He gave me a twenty and I handed him the change. Our fingers almost touched.

'Well, see you in French class,' I said lamely.

He gave me a warm smile and nodded, then disappeared out the door with his plastic bag, obviously meant to be shared with someone else. I sighed and turned to the next customer. *Zach*. Of course.

'Hi,' I said, dropping my usual 'how are you today' greeting to customers. I scanned his items: two tins of dog food (on special), a T-bone steak (of course) and a can of coke (not diet). No doubt who he'd be sharing his dinner with tonight, I thought, the mental image of Dave popping into my head. I almost smiled.

'How's the car running?' He asked.

'Fine. That's eighteen dollars fifty, please.'

He handed me a twenty. I gave him the change, and his fingers closed around mine as he took it. I snatched my hand back quickly and looked behind him. There were no more customers waiting. In fact, the shop was nearly empty as it was almost closing time.

He was still there. 'You've got it bad, haven't you?' His look was almost sympathetic.

'I don't know what you mean.' My tone was icy.

'He's not interested, you know.'

'Pardon?'

'The Frenchman. You're wasting your time.' Zach grabbed his shopping bag.

I felt like exploding but, taking a deep breath, I gave him a frosty look instead. 'Well, please don't let me waste yours.'

I had the satisfaction of seeing Zach redden, but his words took some of that pleasure away. 'Don't worry. Babe, I'm not that desperate.' He turned and swaggered—there was no other word for it— out the sliding doors.

I had gone through about twenty emotions in the last five minutes, most of them unpleasant and most of them due to Zach Mills. Who the hell did he think he was? What business of his was it who I liked? But, I wondered, was it really that obvious how I felt about André? And why couldn't he look at me the way I'd seen Zach once (maybe twice) almost look at me? Life, I decided, was very unfair.

After closing time, I sorted out my till and went into the small room at the back where the staff kept their things.

I liked working at the local IGA. Bob, our boss, was good as bosses go, the staff was easy to get along with and I could live at home, which certainly helped my meagre savings. Mum and Dad had been disappointed I hadn't gone to uni, especially as my marks, while not straight As, were good enough to get in. The trouble was, I didn't know what I wanted to do, except go to France. So I'd taken a gap year, well, several actually. But life, a few parties and a busy social life had pretty much taken care of the first couple of years. Then, my boyfriend got transferred in his job to another state and our relationship, which hadn't been that serious anyway, went with him. That's when Andrè Le Blanc had come to town, and saving for France became, once again, my top priority.

Derek, who worked in the fish and deli section, was also grabbing his jacket in the back room. 'Hey Beth, some of us are going to Bart's tonight, if you're free.'

I considered. I was friendly with most of the staff and we often went out for a few drinks or a meal. Bart's was a popular bar, where they served meals and even had a dance floor you could move around if you wanted to. It didn't look as if I had any other plans for tonight. 'Sure. What time?'

'About eight. You need a lift or anything? I'm the designated driver tonight.' Derek grimaced. We often took turns at that. I considered my unreliable Datsun.

'Sounds good, Derek. My car wouldn't start the other night, so yes, I'd be glad to get a ride.'

'You really should get another car. I know this isn't Sydney or Melbourne, but it's not safe to be in a car like that, even here.' Derek was sweet but, seriously, a bit dull. At twenty-five he had the beginnings of a double chin. By the time he was thirty-five, he'd be general manager of the store and married with 2.5 children. I liked him, but he represented everything I wanted to escape from in this town. There was absolutely nothing between us. He was a good mate and that was all.

I smiled at him. 'Tell me about it. But I'm saving at the moment.'

'Yeah, I know, for France.' There was something about the way he said it that reminded me of Zach.

'Yes, for France,' I snapped, grabbing my bag.

He held up his hands. 'No offence, Beth. I know it's your dream.'

My temper cooled. This was not arrogant, know-it-all Zach; this was sweet, dependable Derek, who wouldn't hurt a fly. 'Sorry, didn't mean to snap. Just a bit tired.' I headed out the door to the car park at the back.

'No worries. See you tonight,' he called as I left the building.

A shower, one slice of reheated pizza and half a glass of chardy later, I felt much better. The embarrassment of Zach seeing me trying to attract André's attention was starting to fade. I surveyed my wardrobe. Just friends tonight, no stress. I selected my second-best pair of jeans and a pink V-neck top that complimented, I thought, my auburn hair (I was a bit sensitive to people calling it red). I slipped into a pair of wedged heels that gave me height and comfort—two for the price of one. I was a shoe person, I had to admit. Some of my purchases over the years had put a dent in the savings account. But this year, I had been very good. I only bought shoes when they were on sale, most of the time.

I was all ready by the time I heard Derek's tentative knock. His clean-shaven face beamed at me when I opened the door. 'You look nice, Beth.'

'Thanks. Let's go.' I was surprised to see there were no other passengers when I got to his car. 'Have we still got to pick the others up?'

'Jake and Lisa decided to go with Kirsty, who has a cold and doesn't want to drink tonight. So it's just you and me. Hope you don't mind.'

'Of course not. But we could have gone with them, saved you the trouble.'

'It might be a bit crowded in Kirsty's car.'

'I guess. Well, thanks.'

'Oh, I don't mind really. I'm not much of a drinker anyway.'

I smiled at him. 'No, you aren't. Dependable Derek, that's you.'

He started the car and we moved off, 'Now, you're just laughing at me.'

'Would I dare? Never. That's a compliment you know.'

'Yeah, right.' He shot a grin at me.

When we got to Bart's, the others were already there. I gave the girls hugs and sat down next to Lisa.

'The usual, Beth?' Derek asked.

'Yes, thanks. I'll get the next round.' He and Jake disappeared in the direction of the bar.

'So, how are the French lessons going? I saw André in the store today. I noticed he went to your check out, lucky girl,' Lisa said.

'Wish I was. Sometimes, I think he doesn't even see me.' I sighed.

'Give him time,' Lisa said encouragingly.

'Who was the hot guy who came after him? I saw you talking. Do you know him?' Kirsty's blue eyes bored into me.

'Zach Mills. He's in my French class.' I tried to make my voice sound bored, as if I couldn't care less, which, of course, I didn't.

'Two hunks in one class. Hmm, think I'll join up too,' Kirsty said, and I knew she was only half kidding. She had a predatory, determined streak in her. Ask any customer who tried to get away with only one purchase in the meat and deli department.

'It's probably too late to join now. We're halfway through the course.' I didn't mean to sound defensive. Perhaps I didn't want any competition for Andrè.

'Oh, don't worry. I'm not after your precious Frenchman. It's the other one I'm interested in. You've no claims on him, have you?'

'None in the slightest.'

I was relieved when the guys came back with our drinks and the conversation took a different turn. We had a few laughs, a few drinks. It was nothing serious and that's what I liked about it. I even danced with Jake and Derek, who managed not to tread on my toes.

It was nearly eleven, when Kirsty grabbed my arm. 'There he is.'

'Who?' My heart raced. Surely André hadn't come here?

I turned around to see Zach standing in the doorway and scanning the room. His eyes met mine and he nodded. But it wasn't me he was looking for. A leggy brunette in jeans that looked like she'd been poured into them, walked towards him and his face lit up. They gave each other a warm hug and disappeared into the crowd.

So, he had a girlfriend. Maybe several. What else did I expect? Zach wasn't exactly short on looks or confidence. There was a type of girl that could be attracted to him. It just wasn't me.

'Damn,' Kirsty said beside me. 'Looks like he's taken. You should have told me.'

'I didn't know. In fact, I hardly know him.'

'Oh well, plenty more fish and all.' Kirsty shrugged and took a sip of her soda water.

I was suddenly feeling tired and a bit deflated. I wondered if Derek would mind if I just caught a cab home. I didn't want to stay any longer, but it would be unfair to ask him to leave this early.

'You want to dance?' Derek was asking.

I could stay that long, I decided. Wouldn't hurt for Zach to notice I wasn't altogether alone, even though Derek was in the friend and not the boyfriend category. Still, Zach didn't know that. Not that I cared.

It was a slow song and Derek's warm, slightly clammy hand took mine as his arm went around my waist. 'Hey, Beth, I was wondering…'

'Hmmm,' I glanced around the room, seeking Zach.

'I've got this thing I'm invited to, my cousin's engagement party.'

Zach wasn't in sight. He was probably snuggled up in a corner with that brunette.

'I was wondering if you'd like to go with me.'

'Pardon?' I switched my attention back to Derek.

'Would you like to go to my cousin's engagement party with me?' Derek's eager face bent closer to mine and his warm, coke scented breath fanned my face. I tried to move back a little, which was a tad difficult since he was holding me so tightly.

'Gee, that's sweet of you, Derek, but…' I tried to search for a reason that wouldn't hurt his feelings. What was going on here anyway? I thought he understood we were just friends.

'It's on the twenty-sixth of this month. If you need the day off, I'm sure Bob would rearrange the work schedule for you.'

'I…'

I heard a voice which was, for once, welcome. 'Mind if I cut in?'

# Chapter Four

'We're having a private conversation here, mate.' Derek shot Zach an indignant look, but Zach wasn't looking at Derek; he was looking at me with an intense, dark eyed stare. I had to admit, up close, he didn't look too bad, even if he wasn't French. He was wearing a stylish white shirt over well-cut dark trousers. There wasn't a cowboy boot or a footy jersey in sight.

'It's okay, Derek. I know this guy. He's from my French class. He probably wants my notes or something. I'll just finish the dance and be back to join you and the others after.' I squeezed his hand gently to let him know I appreciated his understanding.

Derek gave me a slightly hurt look—I was going to have to let him down, but I'd do it gently—and moved off.

Zach pulled me close and, for a few tingly moments, all I was aware of was the hardness of his broad chest and the feel of his arms around me. I knew I shouldn't have had that second Bacardi and coke.

'Notes? On the dance floor?' Zach looked down at me in amusement and raised an eyebrow.

'Well, you took me off guard. And cutting in? What B-grade 1950s movie did you get that from?'

Zach grinned. 'My Gran's got a great selection of the old classics. It worked, didn't it? And you didn't seem too reluctant to change partners.'

'Don't flatter yourself. I was just being polite.' *And getting out of an awkward situation with Derek,* I thought. I didn't want to go out with him, but I still wanted to stay friends with him. I had a feeling Derek wanted more than that.

As if he read my thoughts, Zach said, 'Your boyfriend didn't seem too happy.'

'Derek? We're just friends. We came here in a group from work.'

'Oh yeah, right. You're saving yourself for your French teacher.'

My spine stiffened. Two minutes, that's all it took for Zach to get under my skin. 'I'm surprised you could tear yourself away from that beautiful brunette I saw you with.'

'You noticed, did you? She is beautiful, isn't she?'

I felt like wiping that smug look right off his face. Instead, I said in as light a tone as I could manage, considering he was holding me closely and my stupid hormones would not obey me and be indifferent to his touch, 'Then why are you dancing with me?'

He bent his head till his lips touched my ear, sending a shiver through me. 'Because, Beth, you are even more beautiful.' Okay, maybe at that moment I was willing to let my hormones win. Then he said, 'Also, because that brunette happens to be my sister.'

I stepped lightly, or maybe not so lightly, on his toe.

'Ow! What did you do that for?'

'Sorry,' I said sweetly, 'Didn't watch where I was going.'

'Yeah, right. You fight dirty, don't you? But, that's all right, I'll get you back.'

'I don't know what you mean.'

'Babe, you know exactly what I mean.' He pulled me a little closer.

Why I didn't leave the dance floor right then, I don't know. I really didn't like Zach Mills. He was not just small-town and unsophisticated; he was also plain annoying. But when he was holding me, all those thoughts flew out of my mind—until the next time he made me as mad as hell, which was sure to happen soon.

The song ended, but Zach kept his arm around my waist. 'Let's go to the bar for a drink,' he said.

But whatever craziness was in my mind had settled and, more importantly, I had thought of a good reason I couldn't go with Derek to his cousin's engagement party.

'I need to get back to my friends,' I said.

'They can do without you for a few minutes,' Zach persisted.

I disentangled myself from him. 'I came with Derek. I can't be totally rude. Thanks for the dance.' I left him looking more than a little irritated. Did this guy think he was such a chick magnet no girl could say no to him? Think again, *Babe*.

I went back to the table and Kirsty pounced on me immediately. 'I thought you said you didn't know him?'

'I don't, not really.'

'Sure didn't seem like it when you were dancing. You also said you weren't interested in him?' Kirsty's tone was accusing.

'I'm not.' Oops, Derek's glum face immediately lightened.

'I wonder what happened to that brunette he was with,' Lisa said.

'Oh, that was his sister, not his girlfriend.' Interrogation or what? That's the trouble with good friends, they're nosey.

Kirsty gave me a broad smile and even Lisa looked mildly interested. 'So, how about an introduction?' Kirsty asked.

'Sure, no probs. Next time I see him and you're with me.'

'No time like the present.' Did I say Kirsty was persistent? She was more like a carpet snake that strangles its victims with a death grip. She never lets go.

'Kirsty,' I said, trying to be patient, 'I can't just march over to him with you and say "Here's my friend, Kirsty, she's got the hots for you".'

'Well, you could be more subtle than that. We could go up to the bar and you could, you know, look over in his direction.'

I shook my head. 'Zach probably wouldn't come over anyway. I kind of let him know I wasn't interested in him.'

'Some friend you are,' Kirsty lapsed into a sulky silence.

Jake, looking thoroughly bored by the conversation, said, 'I'm going to the bar. Anyone want another drink? Derek, you coming?'

'No, I'm good for the moment.'

As Jake went to the bar and Lisa started to talk to Kirsty about a movie she wanted to go to, Derek turned to me and said quietly, 'Have you thought about the twenty-sixth?'

'Thanks for the invite, but my parents are coming back from holidays on that day and I really should be there to see them.' They weren't coming home till the following week, but Derek didn't need to know that.

'Oh.' His face fell and he looked like a sorrowful puppy. I felt guilty, but it would be worse to encourage him when I knew it was never going to lead anywhere.

'I'm feeling a bit tired, Derek. I think I might go home…no, you stay with the others. I'll catch a cab.'

'No, really, Beth, I'm ready to go too.' Ever the gentleman was Derek. He'd make some girl a great boyfriend, but not me. 'Hey,' he said, 'Maybe we could go to a movie sometime?'

Time to set the record straight. Lisa and Kirsty had gone to the Ladies, so we were alone.

'Listen, Derek, you're a good friend and I really like you, but that's what I want us to stay, friends.'

'Friends go out.'

'Sure they do, like now, with other friends. But Derek, I don't want to take it any further. I'm sorry. No hard feelings?'

He managed a small smile, 'Sure. No worries. I just thought we might have a few laughs together, no pressure. And I didn't think there was anyone else, unless it was that Zach guy.'

'Him?' I managed a light laugh. 'Not in a million years. Anyway, I'm going to go now. Say good-bye to the others for me.'

'No reason I can't drive you home, Beth.'

I imagined his kindly, yet disappointed, face as we drove home together and I was afraid I might give in because I felt sorry for him. I liked him too much to do that.

'Don't worry, it's cool. You stay and have fun.' I grabbed my bag. 'See you at work on Monday.' I left him looking dejected.

Truth be told, I was a bit down myself. I had a feeling things were going to be awkward at work for a while. Kirsty was none too pleased with me, and Derek would probably avoid me at work. As for Zach, he managed to press all my buttons without even trying. And Andrè seemed as far away from appreciating me as ever. Add to that, it was pouring rain when I went outside to call an Uber.

I was about to reach inside my bag, when I heard the door behind me whoosh open and a hand lightly touch my shoulder. 'I thought you were with your friends? Haven't you got a ride home?'

I turned to see Zach. 'I was with them, but I was feeling tired, so I decided to go home.'

'No need to call a cab. I'll take you home.'

'I'm fine,' I said, remembering I'd said this once before when my car wouldn't start, and he wouldn't take 'no' for an answer. I reached in my bag to grab the phone.

'It's on the way. If you're worried about my drinking, don't. I rarely drink when I'm out. I've been on coke and water all night.'

'How do you know my house is on the way?'

'Just about everything in this town is on the way.'

I had to laugh. 'That's true.'

'Stay here. I'll bring the ute round to the front so you don't get wet.'

'What about you?'

He shrugged his shoulders. 'Don't worry me. I'll only be a few minutes.' He dashed into the rain, heading towards the car park.

Why couldn't I say 'no' to him, when it had been so easy to say it to Derek? I was puzzling over this, when the door opened again and Derek came out.

'Look at this rain, Beth. I insist on taking you home. Cancel your cab.' Derek being authoritative? Who would have guessed?

At that precise moment, the ute pulled up in front and Zach leaned over and opened the door. Talk about timing. I would have rather gotten soaked than to have seen the look on Derek's face when I said, 'Thanks, Derek, but I've got a ride.' I lifted my shoulders and said, 'It's on his way.'

I got into the ute quickly and winced when I looked back at him. I suspected we weren't even going to stay friends after this.

'Was that the guy you were dancing with? What did he want?' Did I detect a slightly hostile note in Zach's voice?

I was over all this. Bed and a long sleep seemed a wonderful alternative at the moment.

I buckled my seat belt, leaned my head on the headrest and closed my eyes. 'Don't ask,' I said, as we took off.

Zach pulled up in front of the old Queenslander where my parents and I lived. It had originally belonged to Gran, Dad's mum, but she had died about ten years ago and, since then, my parents had renovated it so that it still had charm but was much more comfortable. To me it was home, the place where I could shut the rest of the world out when it got on my nerves. I didn't know how I felt about Zach seeing where I lived. Somehow it was bringing our relationship—*relationship?* Well, acquaintanceship—to a level that was bordering on personal.

He looked at the wide, wrap-around verandah, where I had left the outside light on. 'Nice place,' he said. 'You live here with your parents?'

'Yeah, but they're on holiday at the moment.' As soon as I said that, I wished I hadn't. Zach didn't need to know I was on my own, though it wouldn't make any difference, because I wasn't going to invite him in or anything.

The rain had stopped and, for that, I was grateful. 'Well, thanks for the ride and all,' I said, opening the door and getting ready to hop out of the ute.

'What's your hurry?' He said, placing a hand on my arm. I hated that my nerves tingled with his slightest touch.

'It's late and I'm tired,' I said, as he leaned closer and brushed the hair from my face with his other hand.

'Then, I'd better say goodnight,' he said softly, and he looked at me with a question in his eyes.

I looked back at him, willing myself to move, but I couldn't. What was it about Zach, that despite all the logical reasons I could think of, they seemed to disappear when I was near him?

He moved a little closer to me. 'I'd like to kiss you, Beth. But, if you don't want me to, just say the word.'

I was silent for a moment. I had to admit I was tempted, just to see what it would be like. I gave him a smile.

'I'm going to take that as a "yes",' he said and bent his head, brushing his lips softly against mine.

I swear I didn't mean to kiss him back, but somehow, I must have because he was kissing me again and this time his mouth pressed firmly against mine. Obviously, Zach had kissed a few women in his life because his technique was just about perfect. I closed my eyes and felt my traitorous lips open to his. For a long moment, all I could think about was how wonderful he felt and how I wanted it to go on and on. Zach's arms encircled me and I wound mine around his neck as I felt the warmth of his broad chest and breathed in his clean scent of soap and aftershave. His tongue found mine and heat welled in my stomach. I pressed closer to him and his kiss deepened. Something suspiciously like a moan escaped my lips. His hands found my face and cupped it as he gently lifted his head. His eyes were pools of darkness and his breath was short. All I knew was that I wanted him to go on kissing me. Maybe I would ask him in for one coffee.

But his next words surprised me. 'That's what you call a French kiss, Beth, and I do it way better than the French. So, by the way, do you.'

'What?' I jerked back from him. 'Of all the arrogant, conceited things to say...' I was lost for words. He had completely ruined the moment.

Zach grinned at me, 'Dream about that instead of André Le Blanc when you go to bed tonight, Beth. At least that kiss was real. And there's plenty more where that came from.'

I could have slapped that stupid grin off his face, except that I was too much of a lady. 'If you think for one moment, Zach Mills, that I will ever let you kiss me again after that remark, you're the one dreaming. You're a jerk.'

I jumped out of the ute and slammed the door. I turned my back, and without a glance backward, strode up the path to the porch steps. The stupid man didn't leave, but stayed parked in his ute while I fumbled with my key and opened the front door. What? Did he think I would relent and go back to him? He could think again.

Once inside, I slammed the door and locked it again, collapsing against it. Only then did I hear the ute slide away into the night.

# Chapter Five

The butter sizzled in the pan as I poured in the mixture. I let the batter spread to the sides of the small skillet and poised, spatula in hand, to lift it delicately along the edges as it firmed. A few minutes later, I placed a perfect French crepe on my plate. Then, I poured in the last of the mixture and repeated the process. Placing a few raspberries and a small dollop of cream on each one, I rolled the crepes delicately. Voilà, perfection.

I poured a coffee from the urn and sat down at the kitchen table to enjoy my feast. Every Sunday, my day off, I practised my French cooking. Mum and Dad were usually appreciative of my efforts but, now that they were away, I had to make things that were simple and small. Crepes weren't exactly slimming, but then, I reflected, most French women were thin, so if I ate like them, I surely wouldn't put on too much weight.

I picked up my much-thumbed guidebook to France and took a sip of coffee. Whenever I felt stressed, I found it soothing to plan the itinerary for my trip. I had, of course, gone over it many times, sometimes putting in slight variations of where I would like to go. Doing this never failed to renew my determination to get there one day soon. After breakfast and the load of laundry I had to do, I had planned a relaxing afternoon watching Amelie with Audrey Tatou—in French of course, but with subtitles. Then I would take a long, luxurious bubble bath, apply a small dab of Channel No. 5, put on my silk pyjamas, and reread *The Da Vinci Code*, because I especially liked the beginning when they were in Paris.

Yes, I had my perfect Sunday just about planned and there was no way I was going to let any thoughts of Zach Mills intrude my peace. I would not think about that humiliating experience in his ute last night where I forgot myself and allowed him to kiss me. Or his totally asshat remarks after. I stabbed a piece of crepe and the cream came shooting out on my tee shirt. Grabbing a serviette, I wiped it off, while I made a resolution to have nothing more to do with that smug, self-important, overbearing *bogan*. There was no other word for him.

Instead, I turned my thoughts to André. I would really impress him this week with my improvement in French. Perhaps instead of reading *The Da Vinci Code*, I would go on those websites and practise my conversational French. Yes, I would try a few phrases out and then roll them off at

French class, much to his amazement and admiration. He would be so impressed he would ask me out for coffee and from there…well, at last he would see me, Beth Jenkins, as the soul mate he had been searching for.

I lost myself in misty, rosy dreams of sharing a glass or two of Bordeaux, and then his lips gently touching mine, our kiss deepening and…what the hell was Zach Mills doing in my daydream! It was André who was supposed to be kissing me and not Mr High and Mighty, who thought he was God's gift to women.

Annoyed, I got up and scrapped my barely touched breakfast in the bin. Damn that man, he'd managed to ruin my breakfast and he wasn't even here. Work was what I needed, so I plunged myself into doing the laundry and a few other household tasks.

A couple of hours later, I felt much better and ready to flick on the DVD. It was overcast and almost cool for this time of year. A perfect day to snuggle up on the couch and veg out. I had only just gotten past the credits when my phone rang.

'Beth, what are you doing?' It was Liz, probably the only person from work who was still talking to me. Oh, and Jake. I still felt guilty about Derek. And really, if I had let him take me home last night, it couldn't have been nearly as disastrous as letting Zach drive me. Perhaps I should have introduced Zach to Lisa after all.

'Nothing much. I was just going to watch Netflix. Why? You want to come over.' It might be nice to have a distraction from my thoughts.

'Yeah, maybe. Or we could do something.'

'What did you have in mind?'

'Let's go for a coffee.'

I thought of the couple of places in town where we could go and none of them appealed to me. 'Hmm, I dunno.'

'Not here. Let's go for a drive somewhere. How about Maleny? There are a few nice cafés there. It's not too far to drive.'

I thought of the small, scenic town that had a lot of specialty stores, including a really great cheese shop where I could pick up some Brie or Camembert. 'Sure, sounds like a plan.'

'Great. I'll pick you up in about an hour. We'll go in my car.'

Not even my friends had much confidence in my battered vehicle. But perhaps a break would be good. I put my original Sunday plans on hold. At least I wouldn't be thinking about a certain person and how annoyed he made me feel.

An hour later, we were heading up in the mountains to Maleny. The sun had decided to show and it was turning out to be a beautiful afternoon. Lisa and I sang along to a pop song on the radio, belting out the chorus and laughing in between. I really liked Lisa. She was uncomplicated and fun. I liked Kirsty too, but she was more high maintenance. She was a gym junkie with an iron will. Coffee with her would be black, decaffeinated and absolutely nothing else. With Lisa, I knew I could enjoy a brownie or caramel slice with my cappuccino and not receive a full breakdown of its non-nutritional ingredients and how many hours of cardio I would need to do to work it off. Lisa had a more comfortable personality.

As we neared Maleny, Lisa turned down the radio and asked, 'What happened with Derek last night? He seemed in a really ratty mood after you left.'

I debated how much I should tell Lisa. 'He was annoyed that I didn't go home with him, I think.'

'Why didn't you?'

'I was tired and wanted to go home, but I didn't feel like making him leave early.'

'You know he wouldn't have minded. He's got a thing for you.'

'So I discovered last night. He's a nice guy and all, but I just don't feel that way about him.'

Lisa nodded sympathetically. 'That's too bad, for Derek that is. What about the other guy you were dancing with? Zach, is it? Anything going on there? I promise, I won't tell Kirsty.' She shot a grin at me.

I took a moment to think. Nope. I decided I wouldn't mention everything that had happened with Zach last night, even to kind, nonjudgmental Lisa. She might think I was interested in him, which I definitely wasn't. 'Nothing to tell,' I said. 'He's in my French class, that's all. But he has an ego the size of an entire footy team after they've won a Grand Final. He's not my type at all.'

Lisa sighed then said, 'He sure is hot, though. No wonder Lisa wanted an introduction.'

'Is she still mad at me?'

'I wouldn't say mad, just, well, you know Kirsty…'

'So she's still mad. Oh well, she'll get over it.' I shrugged, not really too bothered. Kirsty arced up quickly, but she also got over things after a while. And she didn't hold a grudge. There were some good points about Kirsty.

We were approaching the main street of the town with its restaurants, gift shops and art galleries. We spotted a café that overlooked the valley. I'd been there once before and I knew the coffee was good and the cakes were even better. Lisa pulled into a parking spot and, within a few minutes, we were seated on the back balcony that had a picture postcard view. We were lucky to get a seat at all as the place was nearly full.

My hardly touched breakfast seemed a long time ago, so I eyed the menu eagerly. After I made my selection—

chocolate gateau and a latte—I glanced up and nearly dropped the menu. André and another guy had entered and were looking around the now full café. I caught his eye and he smiled.

'Hello, Beth, how are you?' He said in that charming French accent.

'André, what a lovely surprise to see you here.' I tried, I really did, not to gush.

'Yes, we came up for a drive and thought we'd stop for coffee, but it seems full.'

He looked around.

I had a sudden inspiration. Lisa and I were sitting at a table for four. I was sensing she would not exactly be averse to sharing our table with two hot men.

'Why don't you join us?'

He hesitated. 'I could not impose.'

Lisa, wonderful Lisa, chirped, 'Please do. We've loads of room.'

Andrè looked at his friend, who shrugged and said, 'Why not.'

'Thank you, that's very kind. Please, let me introduce you to Paul. He also works at the Tafe.'

Paul was a little shorter than Andrè, sandy haired and cut. I could sense Lisa's interest already.

'Hi, pleased to meet you. This is my friend, Lisa.'

As they sat down, I glanced over at Lisa, who flashed a wide smile at me. How sweet was this afternoon turning out. And how glad I was that I had taken Lisa up on her suggestion to come here!

'So, Paul, what do you teach at Tafe?' Lisa asked.

'Motor Mechanics.'

I looked at him in surprise and wondered what on earth he and someone as cultured as Andrè would have in common. But then, Andrè probably didn't know many people yet and they did work at the same place.

'I've been practising my French on some of those interactive websites,' I said, turning to Andrè.

'You certainly are one of my most enthusiastic students, Beth.' He gave me a warm smile.

'Beth loves all things French,' Lisa said.

'Is that so?'

'Yes, one day I'm going to travel there. I've been planning it for quite a while.' No need to mention my meagre savings, and the timing wasn't quite right to tell him I planned on us going together, when we got to know each other a little better.

'It is a beautiful country, but then, so is Australia.'

'Too right,' Paul said. 'I've been telling Andy here he should see a bit more of our lucky country.'

'I plan to as soon as the *vacances,* sorry, holidays, come. I would love to see the Sydney Opera house and Bondi Beach.'

'The Sunshine Coast, mate, is right on our doorstep. Noosa's better than any beach you'll see down south. Isn't that right, girls?'

'Oh, yes,' Lisa said, seeming to hang on every word that came out of Paul's rather broad mouth.

'Australia is beautiful,' I conceded. 'However, every Aussie needs to get out and see a bit more of the world, and France is such a cultured place.' I looked over at Andrè for his agreement.

To my surprise, he said, 'I guess the grass is always greener on the other side of the gate. I couldn't wait to come to Australia. It is so clean and I love these wide spaces and lovely people.' He smiled at me most charmingly. I have to admit my heart did a little dance.

'You've got the right of it, mate,' Paul said, clapping him on the back. 'No better place in the world. Now I'm sure France is a fine place. But give me steak any day over frog's legs. No offence, Andy.' He laughed at his own terrible joke and Andrè gave him a polite smile.

Did I think Zach was a Neanderthal? Paul made Zach look like one of those nerdy scientists from The Big Bang TV show in comparison. I looked over at Lisa, who was still rapt. Obviously, the stars in her eyes interfered with her sense of hearing and taste.

Thankfully, our food came, and I was spared the sound of Paul's voice as he tucked into a BLT accompanied by a Coke. Andrè had a pot of Earl Grey tea and a whole grain muffin. No doubt this would be the last road trip he would take with Mr Motor Mechanic. Perhaps, he would go with me instead. I sent him an inviting smile over the rim of my latte.

We chatted more about France and he told me he came from a small town just north of Paris, and that he had been over here only about three months. He was here for a year, and then he would be returning to France. Oh well, a lot can happen in a year, and that would give me time to save.

Perhaps it would have been different had there only been the two of us, and we would have been able to engage in real, deep, meaningful conversation. However, he did have to be polite and talk to Paul and Lisa. In a time too short to be believed, they were getting ready to go, and no amount of my trying to prolong the conversation seemed to be working.

'Thank you so much, ladies, for sharing your table. It has been a delight to meet you, Lisa. Beth, I'll see you in class, eh?'

I nodded enthusiastically.

'Yeah, thanks girls. See you around,' Paul said.

And then they were gone.

'Wow, that Paul. He's something.'

'Yes, something that should be seen in a freak show.'

Lisa looked at me reproachfully, 'That's a bit harsh.'

I sighed. 'I know, but honestly, Lisa, did you actually listen to him? And that joke about frog's legs!'

'Okay, so he's not Einstein. He's a good, basic Aussie bloke. Nothing wrong with that.'

'Not Einstein? He couldn't even spell it.'

'You know, neither of us is exactly a uni graduate.'

'A fact my parents remind me of almost daily when they are home. Yes, I know, but at least we have ambitions.'

'Maybe you do, Beth. I know you're smart and all that. But me? I just want a bit of fun before I settle down, and then I'd like to find someone nice, have children and have a life.'

I bit my tongue before I said 'That's a life!' Beth was sweet and uncomplicated, and maybe she was right—for her. I knew I could never be happy with anything less than my dream, and I wasn't giving it up for anything, or anyone.

We left shortly after that. The afternoon had been better than I expected, yet why did I feel such a sense of dissatisfaction? I had spent an hour in Andrè's company and he had been very nice to me. Yet, that spark I had felt sure would ignite when the two of us were together was missing, on his side anyway. Perhaps it was because other people were there and we hadn't had much one-on-one conversation. Yes, that must be it. Somehow, I would have to get him alone. Then, I was sure things would heat up.

Thoughts of how I might accomplish this plan pleasantly filled my mind on the way home.

# Chapter Six

'Spill on aisle four.' I heard Lisa's voice on the intercom. Gus, the after-school help, scuttled over with mop and bucket to clean up.

'Hi, how are you?' I said, pasting on my plastic smile as I rolled through the next customer's purchases.

I'd had a bad day. Kirsty was still cranky at me and Derek was avoiding me as if I had Swine flu, the Hendra virus and nits all rolled into one. Even Lisa was a bit peeved at me, stemming, I think, from my criticism of Motor Mechanic Paul. Bob had put me on an extra shift for Thursday late-night shopping, and French class this week was cancelled because André was sick. Probably caught something from Paul, whom I noticed had had a sniffle on Sunday.

Nothing seemed to be going well at the moment. Perhaps it was time to look for another, higher paying job. Who was I kidding? Work of any kind was scarce in this town, and I didn't exactly have a sparkly resume to flash about. I had worked here since high school, and the chance of getting anything else was extremely unlikely.

Dad was an accountant and Mum was a nurse. Neither one of them was very happy with what I was doing. But they were decent about it. My older sister, Lauren, was the star. She was doing medicine and pretty soon would be qualified as a doctor. I guess every family had a black sheep, and I was the nominee. But it really didn't matter what I did, I'd never outshine Lauren, so I'd given up even trying. Except for France, that was my dream. Maybe, once I'd done that, I'd be able to figure out the next step.

I seriously considered a bottle, or two, of French Beaujolais when I got off work. I could watch Chocolat, starring Johnnie Depp and make a night of it. After all, I didn't start work until noon tomorrow.

Finally, closing time came and I sorted out my till. Naturally, I was five dollars seventy short. It had just been one of those days. I didn't hang around, because, face it, nobody wanted to talk to me. I got into my little car, looking forward to the time, ten minutes later, when I would be home. I decided on a Lean Cuisine meal in the microwave tonight. This was not a time I felt like having a whirl with French cordon bleu.

Half an hour later, I was settled with my spicy pumpkin risotto and the longed-for glass of Beaujolais, watching Master Chef and hoping to pick up a few points. I found, after all, I wasn't in the mood for Chocolat, no matter that it was a classic.

My phone rang.

'Hi.' A male voice that sounded awfully like Zach's shattered my peace.

'Zach?'

'None other. How are you?'

'I'm fine. How did you get my number?' I hoped my voice indicated that I wasn't pleased, even though my stupid heart jumped up into my mouth. Jeez, I hated biology.

'Got a list of everyone's email addresses and numbers in the class when I enrolled. Everyone did.'

I remembered. It was supposed to be in case we wanted to contact each other about assignments and stuff. At the time, I hadn't given it a second thought. Now, I thought it was a terrible intrusion into people's private lives. 'Hmm, what do you want?' I said ungraciously.

'That doesn't sound very friendly,' he said.

'It wasn't meant to be. What do you want?' I repeated. I still hadn't forgotten Saturday night.

'Well, two things. First, an apology. I acted like a jerk on Saturday night and said some stupid things. I'm sorry.'

'Yes, you did.'

'I'm not normally like that. It's just when things are going well, I do something stupid to spoil them, because I can't believe it's going to last. Does that make sense?'

'No,' I said, though I could sort of see what he meant. I'd done the same thing myself sometimes, self-sabotage, that is. I knew with me it was because I didn't feel all that confident sometimes, but I would never have thought that about Zach, who seemed self-confidence personified.

He sighed. 'Okay, but just know I'm really sorry and it won't happen again.'

'Too right, it won't,' I said, thinking there was no way I'd ever kiss Zach Mills again. 'What was the second thing you wanted to say?'

'I hoped you'd help me catch up with French. After all, you did offer to share your notes on Saturday night.'

'There isn't a French class this week,' I reminded him.

'Yeah, I know. All the more reason to catch up before I get left behind.'

'I think you'll manage, Zach. We haven't done that much.'

'An hour, tops, that's all it will take. Surely you can fit me into your busy schedule.'

There was no way I wanted anything to do with Zach Mills. He was trouble with a capital T. But, damn it, he had come to my rescue when the car was broken down, even though I hadn't wanted him to. I did kind of owe him a favour. I had a mental image of my mother telling me off and not to be so rude. Parents have a lot to answer for.

'Okay,' I said. 'When do you want to meet?'

'How about tomorrow night? It was supposed to be French class, but since it's been cancelled, we could meet then.'

I sighed. 'Fine. Where?'

'How about I pick you up and we go to my place. Dave's been missing you.'

'Yeah, right. Haven't you fed him lately?'

'Now, now, don't be like that. He's friendly, that's all. Wouldn't hurt a hair on your head.'

'Says every dog owner in the world. Isn't there somewhere else we could meet?'

'I could come to your place.'

There was no way I wanted Zach Mills on my territory. At least if I went to his place, I could control when I arrived and when I left. I would give him an hour, no more. 'No, I'll come to you around seven tomorrow. I can only give you an hour. I have an early start the next day.'

'Do you want me to pick you up?'

'My car's fine. I'll come to you.'

'Great, I look forward to it.'

'Right, see you then.' I was about to hang up when he spoke again.

'And, Beth, thanks. I appreciate you giving me a second chance.'

'This isn't a second chance, Zach. I'm only catching you up in French, nothing more.'

'Sure, got you.'

Afterwards, I found myself staring at the TV blankly. Who would have thought Zach Mills would apologise? I didn't want to go, I shouldn't go and yet, a small part of me was looking forward to tomorrow night already.

Nights started to close in early in April, so by the time I rolled up at Zach's house at 6:45pm it was dark. I was early, following the premise that the sooner I got there, the sooner I could leave. The outside light was on and I looked around warily for Dave. I wasn't all that convinced by Zach's assurance that his dog—more like a small horse— was harmless. I stepped out of the car cautiously. No dog in sight. Shifting my French book and notes to the other arm, I closed the car door and headed for the house.

Taking a deep breath, I knocked on the front door. To my surprise, the tall, gorgeous brunette I had seen the other night with Zach, opened the door.

'Hi, you must be Beth. Please come in,' she said. 'Zach's just outside feeding Dave. He'll be in shortly. I'm Charlotte, Zach's sister, by the way.'

'Hi, nice to meet you,' I said. Her long, dark hair skimmed her shoulders, and she was wearing a dove grey silk blouse over Sass and Bide jeans. Black heels and a chunky silver bracelet completed the picture of someone who seemed as opposite to Zach as possible. Perhaps he was adopted.

She led the way down a broad hall to the lounge room, which was comfortably furnished with a dark maroon leather sofa and a couple of armchairs. A thick charcoal grey rug covered the tiled floor, and a couple of watercolour landscapes were on the wall. Obviously, Charlotte must have had a hand in the decorating. I sat down on the sofa and Charlotte took one of the armchairs.

'Would you like a glass of wine or maybe a cold drink? As you can see, I already have one.' She pointed to the quarter glass of white on the coffee table.

'No, thanks. I'm fine for the moment. It's not long since I've eaten,' I added, not wanting to sound rude or standoffish. But wine and Zach Mills would be a bad combination.

'It's really nice of you to give Zach a hand. He's really keen to brush up on his French but hasn't had a lot of chances to practice it lately, especially since I haven't been home much over the last year or two. And, of course, he'd be far too shy to ask for much help in class.'

Zach, shy? Were we talking about the same person?

My disbelief must have shown on my face because she said, 'Oh, I know he comes across as very confident, but that's just a front.' She laughed and added, 'I'd better be quiet, or I'll ruin the good impression you have of him.'

Yet again, another indication that perhaps Zach Mills wasn't the self-assured guy I thought he was. *Interesting*. But as for having a good impression of him, no worries there, as that didn't exist.

I picked up on another tidbit she had mentioned. 'So, you don't live here all the time?' I asked.

'No, I live in Sydney, but I fly up every now and then to see how my kid brother is going, especially since our parents died.'

'Oh, I'm sorry. Your parents passed away?'

Her face clouded. 'Yes, but it's been a few years now. It was hard at first, especially for Zach, but we've coped.' She made an effort to smile. 'Tell me about you, Beth. What do you do?'

I hated when people asked me that question because my ambitions weren't immediately obvious to people who didn't know me. 'I work at the local IGA.'

She nodded politely, clearly unimpressed but not stupid enough to say something like—'Oh, that must be interesting'—because obviously, it was not.

At that point, I heard a door open at the back and footsteps came up the hall. This was one of the few times I was relieved to see Zach. His face brightened when he saw me.

'Beth, you came.'

Did he think I wouldn't? I wasn't quite that rude.

'I see you've met Charlotte.' He sat down next to me, laying a casual arm across the sofa back, a gesture that managed to stretch his dark tee shirt even more tightly across his broad chest.

'Yes, I've been telling her all sorts of things about you, Zach.' Charlotte smiled at him wickedly.

'Don't believe a word she says, Beth. My sister loves to get me in trouble.'

'How do you know it was all bad?' I asked, raising an eyebrow.

'Oh, well, if she's singing my praises, sing away, Sis. I need all the help I can get.'

Charlotte laughed then stood up. 'I think you'll manage, Zach. Anyway, I have to go. I'm meeting some friends tonight for dinner. It was nice to meet you, Beth. No, don't get up. See you later, Bro.'

As she left and the front door closed, I became aware of how close Zach was sitting to me. And also, how he was looking at me. I edged a little away from him. 'Shall we get started?' I said in as business-like a tone as I could manage.

'Sure,' he said, moving closer. 'What did you have in mind?'

# Chapter Seven

His arm dropped around me, pulling me closer until I could feel the heat of his body and the steady beat of his heart. 'We could pick up where we left off on Saturday night, and I won't spoil it this time. I'm sure there's an awful lot you could teach me, *chérie*.'

For a nanosecond, as I breathed in his clean soap scented, masculine warmth, I was tempted. But then reason and common sense kicked in, not to mention the memory of how Saturday night had ended. Apology or not, I wasn't going there again. And as for him being shy? I thought not. I moved away from him and stood up, placing a safe distance between us.

'I seem to remember you apologising for Saturday night, Zach.' I gave him a level stare.

'Yes, for what I said. But I could never be sorry about kissing you, Beth. It was a memorable experience.' His dark eyes were warm, teasing, inviting—forget it.

I bent down and picked up a large cushion from the chair Charlotte had been sitting in and aimed it at Zach.

It hit him squarely in the face, then bounced off lightly onto the floor.

'Get over yourself, Zach Mills.'

He grinned broadly. 'You know, Beth, it's almost too easy teasing you, but it doesn't make it any less enjoyable.' He stood up. 'Come on, let's go to the kitchen where we can sit at the table and you won't be so temptingly close.'

I grabbed my books and headed down the hallway. I don't think there was a person alive who didn't annoy me more than Zach Mills, and not only did he know it, he positively delighted in it.

I sat across from him at the broad pine table and opened my French book. 'You've missed three lessons and part of the fourth one. So far, we've learned the days of the week, months of the year, some basic vocab, as well as a few common phrases, including how to introduce and describe ourselves. Do you know much French?'

'A little, but I've forgotten most of it. Charlotte's pretty good at it, but she's not here usually.'

That's right, I thought, remembering she had said something about she wasn't here for him to practise with. I could understand someone like Charlotte wanting to learn French, but I wondered why Zach wanted to. I was tempted to ask him, but I didn't want to get into anything personal at the moment. I wanted to get this lesson over with as soon as possible.

I ran over the first couple of lessons, and Zach listened carefully, obviously deciding to behave himself for a while. His accent was surprisingly good, and he caught on very fast. I suspected he knew more than he let on. However, I just ploughed on determinedly, not wanting to get side-tracked from my goal of finishing this quickly.

We were on the last lesson where Zach had to describe himself. Another ten minutes, max, and I would be out of here.

'How about I describe you instead?' He said.

'Red hair, green eyes, pretty standard,' I said tartly.

'Oh no, not standard at all. I don't know if the French have a word for that particular tint of auburn hair which catches the sunlight and glows like fire or those green eyes that change with your mood. I've only got to look at your eyes to know what you're feeling.'

I didn't like the way this conversation was heading. I closed my book. 'I think we've had enough for now. You should be fine in French class.'

'I agree. Let's have a glass of wine and sit down somewhere more comfortable.'

'I've had enough teasing for one night, Zach, and it's getting late.'

'Yes, eight thirty at least. Very late.'

'I've got work in the morning.'

'I'm sure you can manage a glass of wine, or a coffee if you don't want to drink and drive. I'm not teasing now. I'd just like to get to know you better, Beth, no strings attached or hidden agendas. Come on, let's be civil to each other for a change.'

I sighed. It seemed ridiculous to protest any more without sounding immature and rude.

'Okay, a coffee. And I'm quite comfortable in here.'

'Your call.' He got up to put the kettle on.

He sat down again. 'Tell me why you like French so much. And, I am being serious here, no jokes about the French teacher intended.'

I considered a moment. 'I don't know really. From the very first moment when I started to learn French at school, I loved it. It was the one area where I was better than my sister, Lauren, who sucks at languages. She was all over maths and science and a straight A student.'

'I'm sure you would have been okay in other areas, too. You seem pretty switched on to me.'

'Yeah, mainly Bs and the occasional C, or even the occasional A. Average really. Mum and Dad never made me feel badly, or that I was in any way not as good as Lauren. But it was obvious. And I couldn't hate her for it. Lauren's a great sister and she would do anything for me. But I just knew not to even bother to compete academically. So, I started to get into French. French food, French music, French anything really.'

*Including French men*, I thought. It was there between us. I knew he was thinking it, but to give him credit, he didn't say it.

'So why didn't you go to uni and do something with it?' He got up to turn the now boiling kettle off and turned to look at me.

'I probably will, eventually. I just wanted a break from the whole studying and academic thing.'

He looked at me, considering, and I had the uncomfortable feeling that he saw more than I wanted him to. I hadn't realised until just now, how much I resented my sister's success. How, because I couldn't compete, I took myself out of the competition altogether. I couldn't blame Lauren or my parents. They hadn't made me feel badly. I had done that all by myself.

Zach started to make the coffee. 'Milk? Sugar?' He asked.

'Small drop of milk, no sugar thanks.'

He made the coffee and brought it to the kitchen table. 'Would you like anything to eat? I'm pretty sure I've got some Tim Tams somewhere.'

I shook my head. 'I'm good.'

He smiled at me. 'You are that.'

I lowered my eyes from his intense gaze and took a sip of coffee. I wasn't sure I liked how personal this was getting.

'So, your parents, you mentioned they were away.' He sat down opposite me again.

'Yeah, at the coast for a few weeks' holiday. But even when they're home, they're great. We get on really well. I guess I lucked out in the parent department.'

I saw a look in Zach's eyes, and I remembered that his parents had died a few years ago. 'Charlotte told me about your parents. I'm really sorry, Zach.'

He shrugged his shoulders. 'It's okay. It happened several years ago, a road accident that took them both. But there's been enough time to get over it and adjust.'

I wondered if you would ever get over something like that, but I said nothing. We drank our coffee in silence for a few minutes. But it was a comfortable silence.

'How long is Charlotte here for?' I asked, breaking the quiet.

'She's going home on Friday. She has a couple of things on in Sydney at the weekend.'

'She seems nice,' I said politely.

'Yeah, she's the best. I tease her a bit, but we get on really well.'

'Tease her? I never would have guessed.'

Zach's face broke into a grin. 'She gives as good as she gets.'

'I think I realised that. I'm glad someone keeps you on your toes.'

'Oh, you're managing pretty well.' He took our now empty coffee cups and brought them over to the sink.

I took the hint and got up. 'I should go.'

Zach came over to me. 'That offer of wine still holds, or maybe a liqueur? I've heard that Tia Maria goes really well after coffee.'

'Thanks, but no. I'm not really that much of a drinker.'

Zach took a step closer, and I held my breath. He looked at me, really looked, and I felt something turn over in my stomach. 'I'd really like to kiss you again, Beth. And I won't spoil it this time by saying something stupid.'

I closed my eyes. I tried to speak, but nothing came out. What the heck, it was just a kiss. I sighed and opened my eyes, moving closer to him. He bent his head. His lips, so warm, pressed against mine and, without meaning to, I melted into him. He took an intake of breath and his arms went around me, holding me closely. I felt his hips next to mine and my breasts tight against his chest. My arms went around his neck and I pressed against him, fitting my body next to his like a missing piece in a jigsaw puzzle. His kiss deepened and I felt his tongue urging my mouth open. I opened up to him and felt his tongue finding mine. Heat pooled in my stomach and I was lost. My feelings spiralled out of control as I felt the heat rise higher and higher inside me. My hands tangled in his hair and his mouth left mine to travel down my neck. I wanted Zach like I had never wanted anyone else before.

He lifted his head, his eyes deep wells of darkness. 'Not here. In my bedroom, now.'

'Yes,' I breathed, and he grabbed me and practically carried me down the hall to his room. We tumbled in as he closed the door with his foot, and we fell on the bed, his mouth on my neck and my hands on the waist band of his jeans.

'Zach, I'm home,' I heard Charlotte's voice from down the hall. I froze.

'Damn, it's Charlotte,' Zach said, stating the obvious.

In a microsecond I was off the bed. Zach straightened the doona, and I smoothed my hair.

'Um, why don't you go into the adjoining bathroom? It's two-way so you can go out through the hallway when you're finished.'

'Good idea,' I said, and without another word fled through the door. I closed it behind me and leaned against the door, breathing heavily for a few moments. What was I thinking? I felt heat flood my cheeks, but it had nothing to do with arousal and everything to do with embarrassment. Zach Mills, the person that annoyed me more than anyone else I knew, and I just about did it with him. And then, his sister was just seconds from discovering us together. OMG, how was I ever going to live this down?

I flushed the toilet then turned on the water, splashing my face noisily several times. When I was slightly more composed, I took several deep breaths and went out, hearing voices in the kitchen. Zach's sounded remarkably calm. He was obviously better at deception than I was.

I walked into the kitchen to see them both sitting at the kitchen table. 'Oh, hi Beth. How did the French lesson go? I hope my brother behaved himself.'

I caught my breath when she said that but, as I looked at her, I couldn't detect any deeper meaning. She just smiled casually and leaned back in her chair and yawned.

'Oh, pardon me. I'm more tired than I realised, which is why I came home early. But please, don't let me interrupt your lesson. I'm off to bed.'

'No, it's fine. We're done. As a matter of fact, I was just leaving,' I said, wondering at my calm tone.

Zach got up and made no effort to dissuade me. 'Thanks, Beth. I appreciate your help. Let me walk you to your car.'

Charlotte waved a hand at me, 'Good night, Beth. I'm sure we'll meet again.'

I escaped before either Zach or I would say something that might make Charlotte think there was something more than just French going on.

I couldn't get to my car quickly enough. But Zach put a hand on my car door before I could open it. 'Beth, I'm sorry. I got carried away.'

I couldn't look at him. He wasn't the only one. His finger gave my cheek a gentle stroke. 'Hey, you sure are something, Beth Jenkins. When can I see you again?'

I removed his hand and forced myself to look at him. 'In French class, I guess. I'm sorry, this was a mistake.'

'What do you mean? You were there with me, every step of the way. If Charlotte hadn't come…'

'Thank God Charlotte came. Zach, I'm sorry, this is not what I want.' I hesitated then said, 'Everything that happened just got out of hand. I didn't mean to lead you on.'

'Babe, you didn't lead me on. You wanted me and I wanted you. What's wrong with that? We've obviously got the chemistry. Why not see if we've got anything else?'

'But that's just it. We're not suited. This could never work. We want different things.'

He took a step back. 'It's the Frenchman, isn't it?'

I was silent, not wanting to deny it. But truthfully, it had nothing to do with André. It was Zach himself. I didn't want small-town, I didn't want my horizons to end here the way that Lisa would have been happy to accept. In fact, I didn't want Zach.

Zach put his hands on his hips and looked away. 'I see. Well, good luck with your dreams, Beth. And, as for wanting different things, you would't have a clue what I want from life. You've just assumed. But, don't worry, I won't bother you again.' And without a backward glance, he walked back to the house.

I started the car and headed on the long journey home. This was for the best, it really was. I never wanted to encourage Zach Mills and now I wouldn't have to worry about him again. I blinked away the tears that welled, and cursed the hormonal imbalance that had me missing him already.

# Chapter Eight

My life sucked. Almost everyone at work was ignoring me, which made the days long. My social life was practically non-existent, and my goal for getting to France seemed as far away as ever. If the week went by at a snail's pace, the weekend seemed even slower. I could have been going to Derek's cousin's engagement party, if I had wanted. It showed how down I was when I even considered that preferable to my own company. Not even my French onion soup and Pear Belle Hélène made me feel better, even though they were made to perfection. I asked Lisa if she wanted to come over and share the meal with me, but apparently, she was busy. Probably washing her hair or something equally important.

Finally, it was Tuesday again and time for French class, the highlight of my week. I wondered uncomfortably how Zach would behave towards me. I'd felt every kind of emotion since that night of our disastrous French lesson and what followed. I couldn't blame Zach at all because, as he said, I was right there with him every step of the way, and that was what bothered me the most. I had wanted him all right, and if I was honest, I still did. He seemed to awaken every lustful feeling in me, but that was all it was—lust, and I needed more, but just not from Zach. It also bothered me that I'd probably hurt his feelings, or at least his ego. I hadn't behaved well. In fact, I'd handled everything badly.

So, I entered the class feeling anxious and uneasy. For once, André seemed to acknowledge my presence with more enthusiasm than usual. He shot me a broad smile, which cheered me up enormously.

'*Bonjour*, Beth. *Comment allez-vous?*'

'*Très bien*, André,' I answered enthusiastically.

'It was so kind of you and your friend, Lisa, to share your table with us last week,' he said, lapsing into English.

'It was great seeing you there and meeting Paul,' I said, crossing my fingers about that little white lie about Paul. I was determined to be kind. 'Maybe we can do it again some time,' I added hopefully.

'*Bien sûr*,' he said, smiling politely, and turning to greet a couple of other students who had arrived.

That was a promising start, but the rest of the lesson progressed slowly. I kept looking at the door, expecting to see Zach any minute, but he didn't show. Perhaps I had put him off French for good. As we went through the months, seasons and special days, I couldn't help feeling even guiltier about my treatment of Zach. If a guy had done that to me, I wouldn't speak to him again, ever. So why did I expect a different reaction from Zach?

By the end of the lesson, I was back to my earlier feeling of depression. I never even tried to have a last few minutes of conversation with André, like I usually did. Driving home, I wondered if I should ring Zach and tell him I was sorry for the way I'd cut him off. But would that help? I didn't feel any differently. My dreams were still my dreams, and Zach did not fit into them. I didn't want him to think there was any chance of a relationship between us when there clearly was not.

I sighed as I turned into our driveway. Thank goodness Mum and Dad were coming home this weekend. At least there was someone in the world who cared about me, I thought, indulging in a moment of self-pity, that was becoming far too familiar.

Mentally, I shook myself. *Get over it, girl.* Hot tea, a buttered muffin (English, I wasn't in the mood for anything French at the moment) and an old Buffy DVD. What can I say? I was a Joss Whedon fan from way back, ever since my Aunt Jan lent me her box set.

But the old magic wasn't working. I looked at my watch. It wasn't too late to ring Lauren; I hadn't talked to her in ages.

She picked up straight away. 'Hey, Sis. How's it going?' I said.

'You couldn't have called at a better time. I'm brain dead from spending the last two hours studying for a chemistry exam. How are you?'

'Okay. Nothing much happening here. Mum and Dad will be home on the weekend.'

'Yeah, I was thinking of coming home to see them, but honestly, I'm too flat out at the moment, so I don't think I'll make it.'

'S'okay. They'll understand.' I was disappointed though. It would have been nice to see Lauren, who lived in Brisbane. She came home when she could, but she was usually busy studying.

'You know, I thought of you the other day. Uni has exchange students from France here. A couple of them are doing pre-Med. I think our university has sent students over there, too.'

'Sounds exciting,' I said slowly. I had a feeling where this conversation was heading.

'Of course, you have to be enrolled in a degree. But if you, for instance, decided to enrol mid-year, say in a Bachelor's with a major in French, I bet you could get yourself accepted as an exchange student next year.' I knew it. Lauren's agenda was to get me in uni instead of what she thought of as wasting my time in Clearwater Creek.

'I don't know, Lauren. I'm doing all right here. I'll get to France eventually.'

'Darling Beth, I hate to disagree with you, but in what way are you doing "all right"? You know you can't work at the IGA forever, and the years are ticking away. You could have just about finished your degree by now if you had enrolled right after high school. And I bet you haven't even got that much saved for your trip, have you?'

Big sister talk 101. I sighed, having heard it all before. I knew what Lauren said made sense, but trouble was, when she said it, I just wanted to do the opposite. Even Mum and Dad weren't as persistent as she was. Or as bossy. 'I really don't feel like going into this at the moment, Lauren. I just called to see how you were.'

'I'm fine, honey. I'll be a doctor by the end of the year, which was my dream. I know you have yours as well, but you do have to work for them, Beth. They don't just happen.'

'Enough of the lecture already,' I snapped, tempted to hang up on her.

'Okay, chill,' she said, obviously realising she had taken it too far. 'Listen, why don't you come and visit me in a few weeks, when I've finished my exams? We could spend time together, have some fun.'

'Sure, I'll think about it.' We chatted for a few minutes longer, Lauren trying to make up for being the overbearing sister.

When she hung up, I was feeling worse than ever. Yet again, my sister had managed to make me feel like a failure while trying to 'motivate' me. I turned off the DVD player and switched off the lights. It was time for bed and the end of what had been a very long and miserable day.

I was no sooner tucked up in bed when I heard a sound like someone in army boots running across our tin roof. *Possums*, I thought. Nothing to worry about. Even when the outside sensor light came on, I told myself sensibly that possums or some other night creature had obviously set it off. But still, I locked my door and got out my torch from the bedside table. It was heavy, a good weapon. Not that I would need it. I pulled the doona up to my chin and determinedly closed my eyes. I'm not the nervous type, and it didn't usually bother me to be on my own. After all, Clearwater Creek was not Sydney or Melbourne, or even Brisbane. While crime was not completely unheard of, it was rare.

I was just starting to drift off again when I heard a huge crash outside that jerked me into wakefulness. What the...? I cautiously crept out of bed and went to the window. I was glad the wrap-around verandah did not extend as far as my bedroom and there was only one way into it. I looked down at the moonlit back yard that stretched back to the couple of mango trees and the Hills Hoist, where a couple of tea towels moved listlessly in the light breeze. No one was there, but what had the crash been? I listened anxiously for a few tense moments, but the only thing I heard was the beat of my own heart that had jumped up into my mouth.

Then I heard the splinter of glass from the front. *Oh, God.* Someone was breaking in. My mouth went dry. After what seemed an eternity, I managed to move over to the bed to grab my torch and phone. Damn, my phone was dead. I'd forgotten to charge it after I'd talked to Lauren. What the hell was I going to do now? I crept to the bedroom door, putting my ear against it and listening for the sound of footsteps. Nothing. But weren't burglars usually very quiet and stealthy? I searched around for a hiding place in case I needed it. There was only the cupboard, the most obvious place in the world, and I didn't fancy being trapped in there. At least if the burglar came into the bedroom, I could hit him on the head and run like hell.

Then I remembered that my charger was in my bag, which was next to my bed. I scouted over and grabbed it, digging around through make-up, a wallet, a packet of mints and keys before my fingers tightened around the charger. Breathing a huge sigh of relief, I connected it to my phone and plugged it in next to my bed. I waited for a few minutes for the phone to become active again and I pressed triple 0.

'There's a burglar in my house. I need the police straight away,' I blurted out to the voice that answered me. How could someone be so calm when I was in such danger? By the time I'd given her the address and a few details, I was a mess. Any minute now, someone could break into my room wielding some horrible weapon, and this cool, composed voice was telling me the police would be there as soon as they could. She was about as emotionless as an automated call from the library telling me I had an overdue book.

I clutched my phone in one hand and the torch in the other. I guess I would just have to wait it out. At least the police were on their way. But I wanted someone I knew to be there, someone I could trust and rely on. Mum and Dad were away, Lauren was in Brisbane, Aunt Jan lived in Caloundra and Ryan and Rex, the terrible twin cousins (even they would be welcome at this point) were interstate at uni His name just popped into my head. *Zach.*

No way, I told myself. That just wouldn't be the thing to do. It would be so unfair, and I didn't even know him that well. I heard the dog next door starting to bark and a flurry of bats fly screeching from the banana trees at the side. Then, I heard the thump of something that sounded like a cavalry charge across the front porch. That decided it. Instinct took over. He had called me and texted me once, so his number was in my phone. I punched it in.

'Hello,' a sleepy voice said after a few rings.

'Zach, it's Beth.' Even to my ears, my voice sounded shaky.

'Beth?' No wonder his voice sounded unbelieving.

'I…I'm sorry to disturb you but I think a burglar is in the house, and—'

'Now? Have you called the police?' His voice became urgent.

'Yes, they're on their way. I hope soon. But I'm really scared in case they don't get here in time. I didn't know who else to call.'

'Where are you?'

'I'm locked in my bedroom.'

'Stay there. I'm on my way.'

I felt better, still scared, but better. Zach was on his way and somehow that was a great comfort. I crept back to the bedroom door, torch in hand, feeling more confident. After all, help was coming.

There were still no sounds. This was the quietest burglar. But perhaps he had already taken what he wanted and left. I thought of Mum's good jewellery in her bedroom and the stash of money Dad kept in his bedside drawer in case of emergencies. It occurred to me that, as a family, we weren't all that security conscious.

I waited, crouched against the door for what seemed like ages. Then I heard a car pull up outside. Zach or the police? If it was the police, they weren't using their siren. Perhaps they didn't want to scare the burglar off. *Oh, God.* Maybe it was the burglar's accomplice who had come to help him in a getaway car? That sent me into another panic attack.

But then I heard footsteps come up the steps to the verandah and someone pounding on the door, calling out, 'Police, anyone there?'

'Yes, I'm here in the bedroom.' What? Did they expect me to come out with a burglar on the loose?

'Open the door, please.'

Taking a deep breath, I inched the bedroom door open and peered down the hallway. No one was there. I scurried down the hallway to the front door and flung it open. Two burly policemen greeted me.

'We had a call about intruders, Ma'am,' one of them said.

'I heard a crashing sound and glass splintering, and someone running across the porch. There must be someone here, unless they've already escaped. You took a while to get here.' My tone was accusing. I looked around. Where was the burglar hiding?

At that moment, a black ute pulled up and Zach jumped out, covering the ground to the front steps more quickly than I imagined was possible. The two officers spun around, hands on their guns.

'No, it's okay. He's a friend. I called him.'

They relaxed, slightly. By now Zach was on the verandah beside me. 'Beth, are you okay.'

*I am, now you're here,* I thought. But I said, 'I'm okay, but I think the burglar must have escaped.'

Zach looked around then walked down the length of the verandah to the corner of the house. 'Come and have a look at this,' he said.

The two policemen followed him and I trailed behind, still feeling a little jumpy. The lead glass lantern that Mum had insisted on buying because it gave a certain old-world charm to our house, lay shattered over the verandah and beside it was a broken pot plant.

Zach looked at the police, who came to the same conclusion as he did. 'Possums,' said the older guy.

'Sure looks like it,' said the other one.

'We'll do a search of the house, Ma'am, just to make sure. But I've seen this before. Possums can make a lot of noise and do a lot of damage. Must have jumped from your roof onto the light here and knocked it over. That was probably the glass you heard splintering. The same one, or even another one, probably landed in the pot plant here and scrambled off.'

It all seemed so logical now. I felt embarrassed. 'I'm so sorry for calling you out. I really did think someone had broken in.'

The older policeman shook his head. 'As I said, it's happened before.'

As they headed off into the house to do a quick search, I looked at Zach, feeling more embarrassed then ever in having panicked and called him. 'Thanks for coming.'

His expression was unreadable. 'Are you okay?'

'Yeah, I am now. But at the time, I was terrified.'

'When do your parents get back?'

'Saturday, and I will be glad to see them after this. I don't usually get nervous on my own, but that glass shattering was what did it.'

'Understandable. That would spook anybody.'

I couldn't get a read on him. He was acting so neutral. Was he annoyed at me calling him or what? 'Thanks again for coming out, Zach. I really shouldn't have called you. I'm sorry.'

'Why did you call me? I mean, wasn't there anyone else?' His tone was puzzled rather than annoyed.

'Um, everyone in my family was out of town, and you were the first name that popped into my head.' How could I tell him that the very thought of him in those terrified moments made me feel safe?

He looked at me under thick dark lashes, still not giving much away. 'There was no one else? Not even André LeBlanc?'

I probably deserved that, but it didn't make it any less pleasant to hear.

At that point, the police came back from their search of the house. 'Everything appears to be fine. We'll be off now.'

'Thanks, officers,' I said. They both nodded and headed down the steps to their patrol car.

I looked back at Zach. 'Do you want a tea or something hot to drink?'

He shook his head. 'Will you be all right now?'

I wanted to say *no, please stay with me,* but I sensed he wanted to go. 'Sure,' I said. Then I said, 'Zach, I'm really sorry about what happened the other night at your place. I didn't mean to hurt your feelings. I've been feeling badly ever since.'

There was silence for a few moments, and then he said, 'But you meant what you said, didn't you? I don't really fit into your perfect picture of what you want in your life.' He waited for an answer.

I opened my mouth to protest and say, give me another chance. But nothing came out. Everyone wanted me to be what I wasn't, from my parents, to Lauren to Zach.

He shook his head and gave a sound of exasperation. 'Don't bother to answer that, Beth. I already know.' He turned to go. As he went down the steps, he called over his shoulder, 'If you get in trouble again, find someone else to help you out.' And then he was into his ute and gone.

I went back inside, too tired to clean up the mess that the possum had made. I'd do that in the morning. Locking the front door, I went inside and back to bed. As I lay in bed, sleepless and staring at the ceiling fan above, I thought again—my life sucked.

# Chapter Nine

I had the morning off and, after I cleaned up the mess the possum had made, I decided to give the house a tidy up in preparation for my parents' return. It was good to have something active like vacuuming and dusting to do rather than think. Usually reluctant to do this sort of thing, I threw myself into a frenzy of cleaning. By noon, everything was sparkly and clean enough, even for my mother.

I was now tired and ready to enjoy a coffee and a cream cheese bagel for lunch. I flicked on the midday news, but my thoughts flitted elsewhere and they turned, as they usually did these days, to Zach. I had tried to make peace with him last night, but it just hadn't worked out. If only we could be friends, that would be great.

I realised that, even though he had helped me out so many times, I knew next to nothing about him. I didn't even know what he did for a living, though I had already pictured him as some sort of tradie or in a job that required a lot of physical movement. His muscular build alone told me that. But what exactly? I should have found out more from his sister. It also struck me as odd that I hadn't heard of either the brother or the sister before. While I didn't know everyone in Clearwater Creek, it was the sort of place where if you didn't actually know people, you'd heard of them, or you knew someone who knew someone who knew them. Both Zach and Charlotte were a few years older than me, I guessed. Zach was probably closer to my sister's age or even a year or two older. You'd think if there was someone as hot as Zach around or as glamorous as Charlotte, Lauren would have heard of them or mentioned them. Even something casual like, 'Yeah, those Mills siblings really won out in the genetic pool'. But not a word. It was intriguing. However, now I'd probably never find out. I wondered if Zach would even come back to French class.

But I couldn't leave it alone. Maybe Lauren might know something about them. It was worth a try. I picked up my phone and sent her a quick text. *Do u know anything about Zach or Charlotte Mills?*

I didn't get a reply straight away, but she was probably in class or something. I decided to get ready for my shift, which started at 1:30 p.m. I was ironing my work shirt, when I heard the buzz that indicated I had a text. I looked at my phone.

*Do u mean the Mills that own Isolde Interiors?* Lauren had texted.

I almost laughed out loud. Isolde Interiors was a chain of fashionable soft furnishings stores that was Australia wide. I had heard the family was based somewhere on the Sunshine Coast, but they would be mega rich and from what I saw of Zach, he certainly wasn't in that category.

I texted back: *Don't think so. Zach Mills is in my French class and lives on the outskirts of town.*

*Doesn't seem like them. U interested in him?*

*Not at all. Just curious.*

So that was a dead end. I finished getting ready for work and put the matter out of my mind.

The store was busy today, which suited me fine because it made the time go quickly. Lisa asked me if I wanted to go to the movies, and even Kirsty said she would come, so I was starting to feel more upbeat. I had tried to act normally with Derek, but he was still acting all mannerly and formal, as if I were a customer and not someone he had known for nearly three years. *Can't win 'em all.* It seemed where men were concerned, I was Miss Unpopular at the moment.

I finished my shift at 6:00 p.m. and arranged to meet the girls at the local cinema around 7:30 p.m. After slipping into my comfy jeans, oldish jade top and flats, I put minimal makeup on. I was going to have a nice time with the girls, regain some ground with them, and totally forget about men in general.

We decided to go to a rom com, certainly not something we could get any guys to go to, at least not any guys we knew. *And that probably included André*, I thought, who seemed pretty masculine to me, but just not in an obvious macho way like someone else I knew. Oops, wasn't going there. I turned my attention to the movie, which was light and funny, just what I needed tonight.

'You know,' I said to Lisa, 'this is nice, just being with you girls.' I passed her some hot buttered popcorn.

'Yeah,' she said, taking a handful, 'sometimes simple is good.'

'Shh,' said Kirsty as she took a sip of her diet Coke. That was a big concession for her as usually she didn't drink soft drinks.

Afterwards, we decided to go for a coffee at *The Coffee Club* around the corner, which stayed open later than the other local cafés. Finding a comfortable booth that had a good view of the rest of the place, we ordered then sat down.

'Can you believe that customer in the Deli today?' Kirsty said, sweeping her blonde hair back with a hand and leaning forward.

'Why? What happened?' I asked.

'He wanted 100g of ham, that's hardly a slice, and 80 g of Jarlsberg. Not worth even cutting. I gave him a look, I can tell you.' Kirsty took things like that almost personally as she was one of the most persuasive workers we had. Customers often came away with more purchases than they had intended after she gave them the benefit of one of her megawatt smiles and hard sells on the cheeses and meats. It was why Bob kept her in the Deli. He wasn't stupid. If she ever did go into sales on a bigger scale, she'd make a fortune in commission.

'Well, someone knocked over the display of Cup a Soups I'd spent ages arranging,' Lisa complained.

'What about the line after line of customers I served today? My feet were killing me by the end of the shift, and I hardly had time to go to the washroom,' I added, not to be outdone.

'Working on the till is tiring,' Lisa conceded.

'But at least you get to meet interesting people,' I said, thinking of the day I'd met André. 'Plus, you get to see what they buy. It says a lot about people.' I thought again about the differences in purchases between Zach and André. That, if anything, emphasised the difference between the two of them. I had been right to let Zach go. We were moving in completely different directions.

Our orders came and I sipped the skinny cappuccino, which I hoped would make up for the buttered popcorn I was beginning to feel I'd had far too much of. We had lapsed into a comfortable silence, when some more customers came in. It wasn't very crowded tonight, being a weeknight. I looked up to see who it was. And nearly choked on my coffee.

Zach came in with a petite girl with jet black hair and Angelina Jolie lips.

Lisa noticed at the same time I did. 'Who's that? Don't tell me it's another one of his sisters.'

'Don't think so,' I managed to say.

'No, not by the way he has his arm around her waist,' Kirsty added.

Zach happened to look in our direction and gave a cool nod before he turned his back on us and led his date to a far corner out of our line of vision.

'Still want an introduction?' I asked Kirsty, half joking. Part of me would have loved to go over there and ruin their *tête à tête*—the French phrase seemed so apt for what I was sure was happening. Another part of me felt like I was in an elevator that had just crashed down twenty floors at the speed of light.

'Don't think they'd welcome any intrusion at the moment,' Kirsty said. 'Did I think he was interested in you? Sorry, Beth. He clearly only has eyes for her.'

I said nothing, but thought, *that could have been me if I had played my cards right*. Only last night, he had been at my house, and if I had said the right thing, perhaps we would be together right now.

But who was I kidding? Zach probably had a string of girlfriends that he kept on standby, and I would have just been one more. Besides, didn't I just tell myself he was not what I wanted? I put my coffee cup down with a slam, suddenly feeling depressed.

'Oh, well,' Kirsty shrugged. 'He's probably out of my league anyway.'

'What do you mean?' I looked at her in surprise.

'He's probably into more educated chicks if he's doing French and all. And he clearly has the looks to get anyone he wants.'

It was amazing how different people's outlooks could be. Never in a million years would I have imagined that Zach Mills was into 'educated chicks'. He had been interested in me, sort of, hadn't he? And there was no way anyone could call me educated, even if I was into all things French.

'We should probably go,' I said. 'Work in the morning and all that.'

'Yeah,' Lisa said, 'I'm getting tired and tomorrow is late night shopping.' She groaned.

We gathered our things, got up and headed for the exit at the front of the shop. Zach and his girlfriend were in the corner, probably gazing into each other's eyes. Other than a quick sideways glance to see where he was, I wasn't going to look any further, that was for sure.

But life is unkind. There had been a spillage on the floor and I just happened to step in it in my most slippery shoes. Of course, I was so caught up in trying to ignore Zach that I didn't see the little yellow sign that told me the floor was wet. In less time than it takes to blink, I slipped and was on my backside, right in front of, wouldn't you know it, Zach and his date. Zach jumped up and gave me a hand up. There isn't a shade of red deeper than the colour my face must have been at that moment.

'You okay?' He said.

I scrambled to my feet. 'Yeah, thanks. I'm fine.'

When he saw I was all right, he gave me a look of amusement that said it all. 'I seem to be in the habit of rescuing you, Beth.'

'Slippery floor,' I mumbled, stating the obvious. 'Thanks again. Please don't let me keep you from your date.' She was looking at me as if I was something she stepped in on the pavement. Ridiculous, that's what I looked like, and I knew it.

Lisa and Kirsty closed their open mouths and came to my rescue. 'Come on, Beth. Let's get you to your car.'

Kirsty took charge of the situation and led me out the door as if Zach didn't even exist. I loved her in that moment and forgave everything she ever said or thought about me.

Once outside, I groaned loudly. 'I can't believe I could be so stupid. What must I have looked like?'

'It could happen to anyone,' Lisa said kindly.

'But it was bad timing,' said practical Kirsty. 'Never mind. He doesn't matter. He's just a guy. Don't stress. Even now, he's probably staring into the eyes of Miss Lipsy and not giving you a second thought.'

I giggled, and suddenly we were all laughing. I felt better. I might have looked like an idiot to Zach Mills, but at least I had my friends back.

# Chapter Ten

Saturday morning and I was making a little ragoût of lamb, baby potatoes, carrots and pumpkin to put in the slow cooker for dinner tonight when Mum and Dad would be home. I had the weekend off, rare for me, so I was going to make the most of it. I planned on popping out to the markets in Eumundi to get some fresh fruit and croissants from the little organic bakery there after I had finished the stew. If the weather held, I might even pack my bikini and head to the beach for a quick swim in the afternoon. Mum and Dad weren't getting home until around five or six, so I had plenty of time.

On my way there, I turned up the radio full blast, mainly to keep my thoughts from drifting back to that disastrous night when I'd slipped in front of Zach and his girlfriend at *The Coffee Club*. My face still burned remembering it. I didn't think I'd ever be able to face Zach again. Now I was hoping he would *never* go back to French class. But what bothered me even more, and this was a surprise to me, was seeing him with another girl. I had thought he was interested in me, at least a little. But it seemed Zach had moved on quickly. Or maybe he just liked to play the field. Whatever. I wasn't sure if it was my ego or something else that was damaged right now. All I knew was that it hurt to think about it, and this damn radio wasn't helping one bit.

Saturday mornings were busy at the markets, even though, at nearly noon, the crowds were thinning. I made my purchases quickly and decided to go for a coffee, when I saw an Isolde Interiors store on the main street. On impulse, I ducked inside. Perhaps I'd see something nice to buy Mum for Mother's Day. The shop was small but stylish, going for an autumn theme with gold and orange pillows and scarlet throws. The young sales assistant shot me a hopeful smile, but I pre-empted her question by saying, 'Just having a browse, thanks,' so she politely withdrew and left me alone. I was debating whether to choose a small, coloured glass vase or a set of place mats with Impressionist reproductions on them, when I heard a voice behind me say, 'Beth?'

I turned and saw Charlotte Mills, immaculate in grey trousers and a pink tailored blouse.

'Charlotte, what a surprise. You're visiting again?' I managed to say. She was the last person I expected to see, but at least it wasn't Zach, though I was pretty sure he wouldn't be caught dead in a shop like this.

'My weekend freed up, so I thought I would fly up. I love to get home when I can. How are you?'

'Good. Great,' I said, trying to sound perky. No way did I want her telling Zach she'd seen me and that I had looked depressed.

'Hope you're keeping that brother of mine out of trouble,' she said and smiled.

'We're just in French class together, that's all,' I said, hoping she would get the hint that there was zero going on between us.

'Oh, then it was very nice of you to give him that help to catch up.' There was a look on Charlotte's face that said she clearly didn't believe me, but she wasn't going to push it. I wondered what Zach had said, or not said, to give her that impression. 'So, what are you doing this morning?' she said, in an effort to change the subject.

'Just picking up a few things from the market. I was about to have a quick coffee before I headed off again.'

Charlotte glanced at her watch, 'I'm due for a break now. Mind if I join you?'

What could I say but, 'Sure, that'd be nice.'

She glanced over her shoulder at the assistant and said, 'Mandy, I'll be out for a while. Back in around half an hour if anyone calls.' She turned back to me, 'I'll get my bag from the back. Won't be a minute.'

As we walked to a nearby café, I said, puzzled, 'Charlotte, do you work there? I thought you lived in Sydney.'

Charlotte seemed flustered. 'I do live in Sydney. Also, I guess you could say I work at the store, from time to time. I know the owner.'

Something clicked inside me as I remembered Lauren's text about the Mills family. I looked at Charlotte, 'You are the owner, aren't you?'

She coloured. 'To be precise, I guess you could say that Zach and I are major shareholders and manage the company that owns the chain. Our parents started it. It was actually named after our mum, Isolde. When they died, we took over. But Zach likes to keep it quiet and lives a low key, normal life, except that I think he works too hard sometimes. I gather he never told you what he does.'

I shook my head, realising once again that I had never asked him. We reached a coffee shop and went inside. After we made our orders, we found a table and sat down. I was still in shock. Zach Mills owned one of the biggest chains of specialty shops in Australia. Yet, he lived in a modest brick house, drove a ute and had a dog named Dave.

Charlotte continued, 'Zach manages the business here in Queensland, where Isolde Interiors originated and I look after the southern states, where there are fewer shops.

Of course, we have other people to help us, but we like to keep a hands-on approach. It was something we learned from our parents.'

'I see,' was all I could manage to say.

Charlotte tilted her head to the side. 'I'm sure Zach didn't deliberately keep this from you. I just assumed you knew. My brother is such a private person, and he hates all the trappings of a privileged life. That's why he bought his present house a few years ago, rather than live in our parents' house. We mainly use that for offices now or hire it out occasionally for business conventions. Gee, I hope this doesn't spoil anything between you two.' She looked concerned.

'Nothing to spoil,' I said.

Charlotte shook her head, 'That's not the impression I got from Zach. But I shouldn't interfere. Blame it on the big sister syndrome.'

'I know all about that. I've got one, too,' I said. 'A big sister, that is.' But that was about the only thing we had in common. I certainly didn't have a multimillion-dollar empire to run.

'I'm sure she isn't as meddlesome as I can be,' Charlotte said.

'Much worse…not that you are, I'm sure,' I said. 'But she means well.'

'As do I, although Zach doesn't always see it that way,' she said and grinned.

Our coffee came and we started to talk about other things. Charlotte told me how, though she was based in Sydney, she really missed the laid-back lifestyle here and came back as often as she could. 'And not just to help out Zach. I have a lot of friends here still, and it's always nice to get back and see them.'

I told her a little about my dream to go to France, but not quite the extent of my obsession. I didn't want her to think I was a freak or anything.

'France is a beautiful country, especially once you get outside of Paris,' she said.

'You've been there?'

'Yes, a couple of times. Once with friends and once with Zach when we were looking for some new products to put in our stores.'

Zach had been to France and had never told me. No doubt he laughed himself silly at my pathetic plans to go there one day.

We finished our coffee and Charlotte had to get back. 'It was really nice bumping into you, Beth. I hope we can do this again sometime. I hope nothing I said put you off Zach. He would never forgive me for that.'

'No worries, Charlotte. It was good seeing you, too,' I said. But after we parted, I realised that was just what she had done. Zach was a completely different person to the one I thought he was. My fault, perhaps, for having judged him and put him in a box before I knew anything about him. But he had certainly acted the part and had never tried to correct my false impression. And for that, I blamed him. I felt like a fool. I had prattled on about my dreams and ambitions and told him he would not fit in with them, when all along he was a very wealthy guy, who managed a nationwide chain of stores. He had probably been overseas more times than I had been to Brisbane.

Then, I remembered his words after I told him we had nothing in common. He'd said I wouldn't know what he wanted from life because I'd made assumptions. And he'd been right. My face burned as I thought about it. Perhaps the fault lay on both of us.

I decided to go straight home and give swimming a miss. After Charlotte's revelation about Zach, I felt the only thing I wanted to do was go home, eat chocolate and watch movies until Mum and Dad got home. Total escape.

I was going back to my car when I saw André coming out of a bookshop. If I hurried, I could catch up with him. This was my morning for meeting people, wasn't it? Then, I saw Paul come out of the bookshop and they started to walk away together. I slowed my pace. I really didn't want to talk to Paul, too. What a shame Lisa wasn't here to distract him.

At any rate, it looked like Paul had persuaded André to see more of Queensland and was acting as an unofficial guide. It was nice of him, but I would have been more than happy to take on the position if André had asked me.

I wondered if I would ever succeed in attracting his attention, other than the teacher/student thing. I never usually had to work so hard to get the attention of a guy. What was I doing wrong? I always dressed well, was enthusiastically attentive in class, and dropped enough hints to make it totally obvious I was interested in him. Perhaps I should take the initiative and give it one last try. I could ask him out for coffee or something, nothing with too much pressure. Perhaps French guys were used to women being more assertive. I was sure I'd read that somewhere. That made up my mind; I would ask André LeBlanc out. If nothing happened after that, then I would give him up as a lost cause. But I didn't believe that. Once we had some one-on-one time, I was sure we would click. And that would show a certain person, whose name I didn't even want to think, that there were many other fish in the sea besides him.

When I arrived home, I saw Mum and Dad's car in the driveway. They must have come home early. My spirits lifted. At last, things were going my way.

# Chapter Eleven

Sunday family barbecues were a tradition in our family. Lauren found she had time after all to come up for the day and even Aunt Jan and her partner, Alan, joined us. It was one of those perfect April days when the sun was shining but it was neither too hot nor too cold.

Lauren and I helped Mum with the salads while Dad got the barbecue ready, and Aunt Jan set the table outside. Alan was drinking a beer, talking to Dad and giving lots of advice on the right way to cook a steak. Lauren and I exchanged looks and she raised her eyebrows. Typical. Alan was great at talking, but not much else. None of us understood, not even Mum who was her sister, why Aunt Jan was with Alan. But, of course, we said nothing. I guess no family is perfect.

'So dear, how are the French classes going?' Mum asked as she washed the lettuce.

'Great,' I said, chopping the onion and wincing at the stinging in my eyes.

'Here.' Lauren handed me a tissue and took the knife from my hands. 'I'll finish that. My eyes aren't as sensitive as yours.'

I repressed a sigh as my sister took over.

'Why don't you make one of your special salad dressings, Beth? I can never manage to get mine to have the same flavour as yours,' Mum said.

I took the ingredients out of the fridge.

'Did you find out any more about that guy…Zach Mills, was it? You know, the one you were asking me about the other night?' Lauren asked, as she finished chopping the onion and covered it with cling wrap.

Even though Mum didn't look up, I could tell her attention was fully directed on me.

I hesitated. How much did I tell them? 'He might be related to the Mills family you were talking about. But,' I hastened to add, 'I hardly know him.'

'Wow,' Lauren said, 'But didn't you say he lived on the edge of town? I never heard of *the* Mills family living anywhere around here.'

'He lives in a fairly ordinary brick house on a couple of acres,' I said, hoping to put an end to Lauren's curiosity.

'I thought you said you barely knew him, yet you've been to his house already?' My sister spun around, her blonde hair swinging and her hazel eyes boring into me. Even Mum slowed down in tossing the salad, waiting for my answer.

There are times when I could cheerfully strangle my sister. I knew it was a mistake ever to mention Zach's name to Lauren. I put the extra virgin olive oil down on the kitchen bench with a bang, determined to settle this and get her off my back. 'I went to his house once to help him with some French lessons he missed. His sister was there. Afterwards we had coffee and I went home. Since then, I've hardly seen him. There. Satisfied?' I didn't mention what happened after that French lesson *or* that he'd come to our house when I thought we were being broken into *or* that I'd made a fool of myself sliding on the floor of *The Coffee Club* in front of him and his date. Those were things I'd *never* tell my sister, no matter how persistent she was.

'Hmm,' she said, considering. 'He's probably one of the distant relatives then. But he must be interested in you if he asked you to help him with his French lessons. What's he like?'

'Okay. Very typical Aussie,' I said noncommittally.

'What does he look like? Is he hot?'

'Lauren, would you please take the onions out to your father and see if Aunt Jan needs another drink,' Mum said, thrusting the bowl into Lauren's unwilling hands.

She left, but not without a backward glance that told me she wasn't done yet. I hoped she was going back to Brisbane tonight.

I returned to mixing the ingredients for my salad dressing while Mum tidied up the few things she had taken out for the salad.

'Darling, how were you when we were away? Everything go all right?' Mum was more for the roundabout approach rather than the full-on attack. But I knew where she was heading all the same.

'Fine, Mum. No probs.' Then I remembered the night of the possum. I knew I'd better tell her about that because the glass lantern and pot plant were broken and the police had come to the house. 'Well, except some possums landed on the roof and jumped on the outside light, breaking it and the pot plant. I meant to tell you yesterday, but I forgot. And, oh yes, I panicked because I thought it was a burglar and called the police. But other than that, no, nothing much happened.' I said all this in a rush, wanting to get it over and done with as quickly as possible. Thank God Lauren wasn't in the room to give me the third degree.

Mum's reaction was bad enough. 'The police! You never told us. Are you sure it was just possums? Are you all right? Was anything taken? I knew we should never have left you on your own.'

'Mum, calm down. I'm fine. It was definitely possums. The police even said so. And as for leaving me on my own, you do realise I'm twenty-one, don't you?' Sometimes, I wondered.

It took a couple more assurances to make her realise nothing serious had happened. But at least telling Mum about the possums had taken her mind off Zach. I finished making the salad dressing and we brought the rest of the stuff out to the deck, where everyone had gathered.

As I tucked into my steak and salad, I listened to Alan tell us all a long, boring story about some fishing expedition, where he had, of course, been the most skilled fisherman and had caught the most fish. Aunt Jan listened to him in rapt attention. I loved my aunt, but I wondered about her taste in men sometimes. Alan had been on the scene for over a year now and I speculated how much longer he would last. By the looks of Aunt Jan, for a while yet.

Lauren told everyone about her plans for when she finished her medical degree. She hoped to do an internship at one of the local hospitals and eventually do further study in the field of paediatrics. She would too, I knew that. Lauren was smart and focussed and would achieve her goals. I was proud of her.

Then, inevitably the talk turned to me. 'So, Beth, how are you going with your plans to visit France?' Aunt Jan looked at me kindly. Being a new age-y kind of person, she was all into visualising and positive thinking.

'Oh, still working away and saving,' I said vaguely, not wanting to go into details.

'France is a wonderful country,' Alan said, preparing to launch into another monologue, which I was quite happy, for once, to listen to, 'But you know, they have a lot of problems with the immigrant situation. As a matter of fact—'

'I was just talking to Beth the other day about how she could go to uni and achieve her dream of travelling to France,' Lauren interrupted.

Dad looked interested. 'Oh yes, go on.'

'We've been through this, Lauren,' I protested.

'No, we haven't. I just mentioned it, that's all.' Lauren continued, 'She could enrol mid-year in June, do a semester's work, then apply for a travelling scholarship to study overseas as an exchange student in France.' She sat back in her chair, pleased with herself. She certainly had both my parents interested now.

'That's a great idea, don't you think, Beth?' Mum turned to me enthusiastically.

'I...'

'It certainly is,' Dad said. 'You know, Beth, if you did that and needed a little extra help, financially, when you went over there, Mum and I would be happy to help.'

She nodded enthusiastically.

'You can't do anything without a degree these days,' Alan said, weighing in. 'I would have gotten one myself except—'

'I've brought the application forms for the scholarship for you to have a look at. We could go online to see what degree you'd be interested in,' Lauren said. *She was just Miss Efficiency, wasn't she,* I thought.

Aunt Jan gave me a sympathetic look. She knew I hated being railroaded into anything. Mum saw it too, and said, 'Why don't we talk about this later, when Beth has had a chance to think about it. Would anyone like cheesecake for dessert?'

The conversation turned to other topics, for which I was grateful.

After Aunt Jan and Alan had gone and I was helping tidy up, Lauren said, 'Sorry if I was a bit pushy, Beth. You know what I'm like sometimes. I can be a bit single minded. But it's only because I care about you, you realise that, don't you?' She looked at me. I sighed. Mum must have said something to her. But I knew she was right about one thing, she did care about me.

'Yeah, I know. Just give me time to think about it, okay?'

'Sure,' she hung up the tea towel. 'Hey, why don't we go out tonight? I'm not going back to Brisbane until tomorrow. We could go to Bart's, have a drink. What do you think?'

I hesitated, 'Lauren, you're not going to give me another lecture, are you?'

'No, sister's honour or whatever. I promise.'

'Oh, all right. I guess I could go. I don't start work until eleven tomorrow.'

'Great. We'll have fun,' she said enthusiastically.

I wasn't sure that she'd be able to stick to her promise about not talking of my future, but perhaps it would be fun to go out. I hadn't been to Bart's since that disastrous night when Zach had taken me home. Not that I wanted to remember that.

Mum drove us there and we decided we would get a taxi home. 'Don't get your sister drunk,' she said to Lauren.

Lauren rolled her eyes and said, 'Mum, I'm not totally irresponsible. You do realise I'm twenty-five years old, don't you?'

I smiled. They were almost the exact words I'd said to Mum a couple of hours ago. Mum shrugged apologetically, 'Sorry, honey. Can't seem to turn the Mum gene off at times. Have fun.'

Being Sunday night, Bart's wasn't too crowded, which suited me fine. Lauren and I got our drinks and found a secluded table.

'So, how are things with you and Chas?' Lauren had had an on again-off again relationship with her boyfriend for several years.

'Okay, I guess. But, you know, I'm not ready to settle down yet and I think he is. I've got years of study ahead of me and he doesn't really fit into my plans.'

It sounded scarily like what I'd been saying to Zach. My sister and I were more alike than I realised at times.

'But you do love him, don't you?'

She hesitated before answering. 'I don't really know. We have a comfortable relationship, but I've never really felt that zing, like you read about in books or see in movies. Perhaps it's all a lot of rubbish anyway, this being in love stuff. Being compatible is probably a far better measure of how successful a relationship is going to be rather than *falling in love*.'

'Can't you have both?' I thought about how I felt with Zach. There certainly was that zing factor, but unfortunately, we weren't compatible. He managed to annoy me sometimes without even trying. As for André, I felt we would be good together. I wanted that zing factor, but it just hadn't happened yet.

'Perhaps. I just haven't experienced it.'

We sipped our drinks in silence for a while. I wondered why life couldn't be simple. Perhaps, if I was someone like Lisa, who didn't ask much from life except as she said, a bit of fun and then a nice man to settle down with, I would be happier. But somehow, I knew I could never settle for that.

I looked across the dance floor where a few couples were dancing, then shook my head to make sure I was seeing correctly. There was Zach, his arms tightly around the brunette I'd seen him with at *The Coffee Club*. She was snuggled into him as if she would never let him go. I had hoped they were only on a casual date the other night. Now, I knew, this was far from casual. From the feeling in the pit of my stomach, I knew something else, too. I had feelings about Zach Mills, and that was the biggest surprise of all.

# Chapter Twelve

'**W**hat's wrong?' Lauren asked, instantly aware that something had upset me.

'Nothing,' I lied. 'I just saw someone I know, that's all.'

'Who?'

'See that guy over there with the brunette? That's Zach Mills.' Perhaps now Lauren would realise what I'd been trying to tell her earlier. There was nothing between Zach Mills and me, and there never would be now. I'd missed my chance. Besides which, now I knew who he was, I realised he'd never be interested in someone ordinary like me. I'd been a passing fling. Someone to practise his flirting skills on. Just my bad luck they seemed to have worked on me.

'He's a hunk, isn't he? Shame he's with that girl. How serious do you think it is?' She looked at me speculatively.

'Stop scheming, sister dear. I should think you'd know by that clinch how serious it is.'

'Oh,' my sister waved her hands in the air, 'That's nothing.' She looked at them again, 'Seems to me she's more interested in him than he is her.'

'And you know that by, what? The ten seconds you've seen him.'

At that precise moment, Zach looked in our direction and saw us. Did I imagine it, or did he change colour? He certainly seemed to move away a little from his date. I gave him a cool nod then turned back to Lauren.

'Did you see that?' She hissed. 'He saw you and moved away. I'd say there is a chance for you if you want it. He's interested all right.'

'For someone so into maths and science, you have an overactive imagination, Lauren.'

'I know the signs, girl. And so should you.'

'Weren't you telling me a few minutes ago you didn't believe in love?'

'Who said anything about love? What's wrong with a little lust now and then?'

Lust, something else that had crossed my mind. It started to worry me how much my sister and I were alike. My words coming out of her mouth made me realise I didn't actually like the sound of them.

The song finished and Zach started to lead his date over in our direction. Oh, no. This was not what I wanted. That girl had seen me on the floor on my butt, looking like a total idiot. And Lauren was starting to look like an eager mama, wanting to marry her offspring to the rich and eligible bachelor. I knew it was a bad idea to come here. She beamed a smile at Zach when he stopped at our table.

'Beth, how are you?'

'Fine. Good. Never better. Yourself?'

'Not bad. This is Chelsea Bartholomew. Chelsea, this is Beth and…'

'Hi, Chelsea. This is my sister, Lauren.'

Chelsea gave us a bored nod. It was obvious she didn't want to come over and meet us.

'Beth mentioned you once or twice, Zach, so it's good to actually meet you in person,' Lauren said. I glared at her, but she was pretending not to notice.

Zach looked at me with interest. 'Oh. She did, did she?'

I decided to take some initiative here. 'I met your sister, Charlotte, yesterday. We had coffee together. She told me how busy you two were, managing your company and all.' There, ball in his court.

I had the satisfaction of seeing him look uncomfortable. 'Really? She never mentioned it.'

'It's a wonder you even had time to go to French classes. I never realised what a busy, jet-setting life you lead. You should have said.'

Zach lowered his eyes, 'Maybe I didn't think you'd be interested.'

Chelsea was getting restless and it was evident she didn't like the turn the conversation was taking. 'Zach, honey, I'd really like another drink.'

'What? Yes, okay. It was nice meeting you, Lauren. Beth, I think you and I need to talk soon.'

'I'm sure I'll see you in French class. Although, since you've been to France already, I'm surprised you need any lessons at all.' I gave him my sweetest smile.

But Chelsea had had enough and was already dragging him away.

As they left, Lauren gave me a razor-sharp look and said, 'All right, what aren't you telling me, little sister?'

'I need another drink first.' I escaped to the bar where I had a quick shot of tequila, not something I'd usually do, but at the moment I needed it. When I came back with our wines, I knew I had to give Lauren something. So I told her an edited version of the Zach and Beth story, not that there was much to tell. Lauren gave an exasperated sigh. 'What's wrong with you, Beth? He clearly likes you and, whether you admit it or not, I know you like him. And don't try to deny it. It's your sister you're talking to here.'

'Okay. Maybe I like him a little. But, it's like you said about compatibility. I never thought Zach and I shared much in common, and now that I know more about him, I'm sure of it. I thought I was in love with André.'

'You mean your French teacher? Has he ever shown one tenth the interest in you that Zach has?'

'Well, no, but we haven't actually spent much time together. I'm sure when—'

'For God's sake, Beth, when is this obsession with all things French going to end with you? You're not in love with that French guy. You're in love with an idea.'

I have a streak of stubbornness in me. It comes from my father's Irish side. The more you push me, the more I go in the opposite direction. And Lauren was pushing hard.

'You know what, Lauren? I'm fine. My "obsession", as you call it, with France is no worse than your obsession with medicine. It may not be as noble or as well paying, but it's something I am interested in, and you don't have the right to tell me what I should or shouldn't do. There comes a time when you should seriously butt out—and this is that time. You either love and accept me as I am or leave me alone.' I stood up. 'I'm going to get another drink. Do you want one?'

Lauren's eyes teared up. 'I'm sorry, Beth, I've got a big mouth. You're right. And, I do love you. I won't say another word.'

I'd heard that before, but for now, it would have to do. 'Do you want another drink or not?'

'Sure,' she said, not game to say anything else.

I went to the bar and had another short. It was that kind of night. Then, I ordered white wines for Lauren and me. While I was waiting, Zach came over next to me. Alone.

'Beth, I need to talk to you,' he said.

'Where's your friend, Chelsea?' I said, in no mood to give an inch.

'She's gone to the Ladies. You know it's not serious between us.  She's the daughter of some friends of my parents. We've known each other for a while. Occasionally, we've gone out, but that's all.'

'Don't think she shares your opinion there, Zach. But it doesn't matter because it's none of my business who you go out with.' I picked up my drinks ready to move off, but he placed a hand on my arm.

'It matters to me what you think. I know I haven't been completely honest with you.'

'Hah! Understatement,' I said.

'Then, give me a chance to explain. Please,' he looked at me and something inside me softened.

'Go ahead.'

'Not here. Not now. Later. I could come to your place after I've dropped Chelsea off. We're leaving shortly. I'll pick you up in the ute. We could go for a drive.'

Being with Zach in his ute late at night, especially after I'd had a couple of drinks, didn't sound very wise to me. 'I don't think so. I'm here with my sister and she's going back to Brisbane tomorrow.'

'What about tomorrow, then? I just want the chance to explain a few things to you.' His dark fringed eyes had a look of pleading in them.

'I'll think about it. Call me tomorrow,' I said.

'Thanks,' he squeezed my arm and let me go.

I went back to our table. Lauren, to give her credit, didn't say a word and I didn't fill her in on what had happened between Zach and me. Perhaps I'd suggest we go home after we finished our drinks.

A couple of guys came in just as I was drinking the last of my glass of chardonnay. To my surprise, I saw Paul and with him—André! This was getting more like Sunshine Plaza on a Saturday afternoon.

'That's him,' I said to Lauren.

'Who?'

'André, the one with the white tee shirt, tweed jacket and jeans.' On anyone else, what he was wearing might look stupid, but on him, the combination was just right. The French had such a flair for fashion.

Lauren shrugged. 'He looks okay, I suppose. But seriously, if I had a choice between him and Zach, I know who I'd go for.'

'Well it's just as well you don't have a choice, isn't it?' I snapped. 'I'm going to get another drink.'

'I thought you said you wanted to go?'

'I don't want to go quite yet. André might come over and say hello when he sees us.' I got up.

'Beth, is that wise? You've already had a lot to drink.'

If anyone other than Lauren had said that, I might have listened. But her words only made me more determined. 'You want anything?' Of course, I knew she would say no. I ordered a vodka, lime and soda and another shot. It really wasn't a good idea, but I was in a reckless mood. And I needed this for courage because an idea had just come to me. Tonight, I would show Lauren and Zach that André was interested in me, that I wasn't an obsessed fool, and that I was in charge of my own life. I even bought a packet of smoky barbecue chips as well and be damned to Lauren, who was almost as neurotic over junk food as Kirsty was.

I caught André's eye across the room and waved. He smiled and nodded politely but he didn't come over. *Give him time*, I thought. If not, I would put my plan in motion. I went back to the table, sat down defiantly and took a large swig of my drink. Lauren looked at me anxiously but said nothing.

The minutes passed but still he didn't come over. What was wrong with the man? I would have to take the initiative as I'd already decided. Instead of asking him out, I would simply ask him to dance. What was wrong with that? I finished my drink quickly. 'I'm going to ask him to dance,' I said.

'Beth, no. I don't think that's a good idea.' Lauren sounded alarmed.

'Don't be so old fashioned. It's okay for the woman to take the initiative occasionally. He's probably shy.'

'I don't think he's shy. I think—'

'I don't care what you think, Lauren. In fact, I'm sick of hearing what you think and everyone else who wants to tell me how to live my life.' My words came out a little louder than I intended.

I rose unsteadily. Perhaps that last drink hadn't been such a good idea, but I would die rather than admit that to anyone right now. I turned my back on Lauren and swayed over to where André was sitting with Paul.

'Beth, don't!' I heard my sister's anxious voice behind me, which I ignored.

He looked up and I could see surprise written on his face. Something inside me quaked a little, but it was too late to turn back now. 'Hi André, how are you?'

'Very well, thanks Beth. It's good to see you.' He was as ever charming and polite.

I took a deep breath, 'I was wondering if you'd like to dance?' I saw Paul give him a glance and open his mouth about to speak. What was wrong with him? Hadn't he ever seen a girl ask a guy to dance? *Jeez, get with the twenty-first century, why don't you?* I saw André quell him with a look. Of course, he would. He had far more cosmopolitan charm in his little finger than Paul would ever have in his entire life.

'But, of course,' he said and rose gracefully. We went to the dance floor. It was a slow tune, for which I was so grateful. At last I would feel André's arms around me. I hoped Zach was still here and watching. I hoped he felt what I had felt when I saw him dancing with Chelsea. *Not that that was my motivation for asking André to dance*, I told myself.

André was a beautiful, if somewhat formal, dancer as I knew he would be. I wasn't as smooth as I usually was. For some reason, my legs weren't quite doing what I wanted them to do. 'Are you okay, Beth?' He asked me.

'Never better, André,' I said, putting my head on his shoulder. I saw Zach over in the corner by himself. The glance he shot me was murderous. *Good.* I snuggled a bit closer.

'Umm. Beth?'

'Yes?' I looked at him and his beautiful face seemed to swim in front of my eyes.

'I think perhaps you should sit down. You don't seem altogether well.'

My patience snapped. 'I'm fine. Don't you get it, André? I really like you and I've been trying to get you to like me for weeks. What's wrong with me? Why can't you like me?' My voice started to wobble and I felt suspiciously close to tears. Oh dear, I was making a mess of this.

'Beth, I do like you. As a student, a friend even, but there is something you need to know.'

'What?' I felt a traitorous tear roll down my cheek.

'Paul is my boyfriend. We've been going out for a few months now.'

If the floor had opened up right now and swallowed me, I would have been happy. If I could be instantly teleported to another planet, I would have felt ecstatic. If I could freeze time, then rewind it and decide not to ask André to dance, I would have cried with joy and even kissed my sister, who must have seen instantly that my French teacher was gay when he put his arm around Paul's shoulder. That little detail had escaped my memory until just now. I thought it was just some manly Gallic custom and I dismissed it from my mind as irrelevant.

'Oh, God,' times a thousand.

The room began to circle around me. I do believe those barbecue chips were off. They were not agreeing with my digestive system at all. I was not going to spew, I was not going to spew, I was not going to…I spewed. All over the floor, maybe even on André's shoes, certainly on mine and in front of…well, everyone. I felt my knees go weak.

I heard several voices call my name at once, and then I sank to the floor, and my sister rushed over to me.

# Chapter Thirteen

I was never going to drink again—ever. As a matter of fact, I was never going out in public again. Perhaps I'd stay in my room like those adult children, who lived in their rooms for months, years on end just playing computer games and avoiding the real world. Sounded pretty good to me at the moment.

A knock on the door vibrated in my head like thunder. I winced as the door opened and Lauren poked her head through. 'Morning. How are you?'

'What do you think?' I said, not in my most perky tone.

Still in her pyjamas, she came in with a glass of water which she put on the bedside table, then sat at the foot of my bed. 'Mum and Dad have gone to work, so I thought I'd hang around here till I saw how you were.'

'Thanks. I guess I'll live. Though I'm not sure I want to.'

'Oh, it wasn't so bad,' she said consolingly.

'Not so bad! How much worse could it get? I made a complete and utter fool of myself. I can never go to French class again, that's for sure. And as for Zach,' I shuddered and buried my head under the blankets.

'He brought you home, you know.'

I whipped the blankets off my head and sat up straight. 'What? I don't remember that. I thought he was with Chelsea?'

'No, I guess you wouldn't remember. Anyhow, after you fell, I picked you up, brought you outside and you kind of passed out, again. Both Zach and the French guy came out to see if you were okay. Zach said he would take us home. Both he and I got you up and into that ute of his in a matter of seconds. André even offered to take us home as well, but I figured you'd rather it was Zach. At least he's still available. André, I believe, is taken.' She giggled.

I glared at her. 'I don't see anything funny to laugh about.'

'Oh, come on, Beth, you have to admit it was a bit funny. And now, at least you know about André.'

'Poor André, I will have to apologise to him, if he ever wants to speak to me again. I don't know how I didn't realise it before. I'm such an idiot. All those times he was with Paul and his complete lack of interest in me, or any other female that I could see.'

'Don't beat yourself up about it. I wasn't sure myself when they first came into Bart's last night and then I saw

André put his arm around Paul's shoulder, and it kind of clicked. I tried to warn you.'

'I know, I know,' I closed my eyes, trying to blot out the memory. 'You said Zach brought me home. What happened to his girlfriend?'

'She's not his girlfriend, although she would be if she could, I'm sure. He took her home earlier in the night then came back to see you. Doesn't that tell you something, Beth?'

'I don't know. At this point I don't know anything anymore. What about Mum and Dad? What did they say when I staggered into the house last night?'

'They didn't even see you. They were already in bed. So, your secret's safe with me. Though I am open to bribery,' she said and smiled. 'Come on,' she said, getting off the bed. 'Let's have some breakfast. It's after nine o'clock.'

I groaned. 'Crack of dawn. I don't think I could eat anything right now.'

'Toast and tea, that won't hurt you,' she pulled the blankets off me and tugged me up.

'You're a sadist, you know that?' I grumbled.

'Tough love, that's what it's called. You'll feel better once you're up and about. You never were much of a drinker, Beth, so it hit you for six. But you'll get over it.

I followed her out to the kitchen. 'I mixed my drinks. I had shots.'

Lauren winced. 'Never a good idea. Put the kettle on and I'll make the toast.'

*

I decided to go to work, despite my thumping headache. It was better than sitting at home feeling sorry for myself. Luckily, Monday was a fairly slow day and there weren't too many customers. During the break, I sat in the staff room at the back, nursing a cup of coffee. Derek was there.

'Hi,' I said, trying to smile despite the tightness in my head.

'Hi,' he answered in an almost normal tone. 'How are things going?'

Not a question I wanted to answer at the moment, so I said, 'Okay, but I've got a bit of a headache at the moment.'

'Do you want a Panadol? We've got some here in the kitchen cabinet.' He went over and got a packet, then gave them to me.

'Thanks, Derek,' I gave him a grateful look and swallowed a couple.

'So, what's been happening with you lately?' He asked.

'Mum and Dad came home on the weekend, so we had a family barbecue,' I said, thinking that would be a safe topic.

'I thought you said they were coming home last weekend?' He said, starting to look a little hurt again.

Oops, I remembered I had used that excuse to get out of going to his cousin's engagement party. Looked like I was back at ground zero with Derek again. 'Must have got my dates mixed up,' I mumbled.

'It's all right, Beth, you don't have to lie. I know you don't like me.' He sounded resigned.

'No, that's not true. I do like you Derek, very much, as a friend. In fact, I like you too much as a friend to use you to go out with and pretend there's something between us.'

I looked at Derek, thinking how nice he was, just like Lisa. Then a thought struck me. 'You know, Derek, you should ask Lisa out.'

'Lisa?' he said as if the thought had never occurred to him.

'Yeah, she's really cool. I think you two would have a lot in common.'

'Hmm, I don't know. My uncle's fiftieth is coming up soon.'

'Ask her. I'm sure she'd love to go.'

'I'll think about it.' He stood up, 'I should get back to work. By the way, how's Zach?'

I rolled my eyes, 'Don't ask. Don't think there's anything going to happen there.'

'That's the thing, isn't it? The people we want never seem to want us back.' There was a sad note to his voice.

'I don't think that's always going to be the case for you, Derek,' I said softly. But in my case, I thought, truer words were never spoken.

*

I never really expected to hear from Zach, but I had hoped he might send a text or something. Yet, after checking my phone about a million times over the next few days, there was nothing. He said he wanted to explain things to me, but I guess the way I acted at Bart's changed his mind. What did I expect? I'd made a complete and utter fool of myself, and I'd made it clear to Zach I wasn't interested in him.

What did I feel now? When I'd seen him with Chelsea, I'd been jealous, plain and simple. I'd hated that Zach was with Chelsea because I'd wanted him to be with me. That was a sobering fact. I had feelings for him, but they were confused. Was it just lust, or was it something else? He had been there for me every time I needed him, even last night. He was the first person I'd thought of when I believed burglars were trying break in the other night. The few times we'd kissed, it had felt so right. And no matter how hard I tried, I couldn't seem to get him out of my head.

But I believed we were incompatible. And, perhaps we were, but not for the narrow-minded reasons I'd given him and myself. I judged Zach before I knew him. And I'd done that with others: Andre, Paul, and even Lisa. I didn't like myself very much at the moment.

And another thing, although it burned me to admit it, my sister had been right. I'd never been in love with André; I'd been in love with an idea. I hadn't even bothered to get to know him well enough to realise he was gay. He'd always been polite, pleasant even, and no doubt had even tried to send me signals that I'd chosen to ignore. Poor guy, he was probably just as embarrassed as me about that night, but he certainly handled it better.

I had a lot to think about. I didn't go to French class that week. I just couldn't face André. As a matter of fact, my love of all things French had taken a big hit. I took down my reproductions of Toulouse Lautrec, put my French cookbook at the back of my bookcase, and threw away my tattered Guide to France. Then, I opened my laptop and went to the websites of several universities to see what degree courses they offered.

There was one more thing I had to do. I didn't want to, but I knew it had to be done. I had to face Zach, even if it was just to thank him for taking me home that night. It was obvious he wouldn't contact me again. I'd burned my bridges there. But I needed to tell him I was sorry, sorry I made snap judgements about him, sorry I used him (imagine phoning him in the middle of the night and then when he came, still acting like he didn't mean anything to me) and most of all, sorry I made him think he wasn't good enough for me.

He had a few things to explain to me, too. Like why he hadn't told me he was the owner of an Australian wide chain of stores or that he had been to France several times and probably knew more about it than I would ever know.

But it was my turn to take the initiative, and this time with the right guy.

I waited until Friday night to drive to his place. I dressed with care in my best jeans and the lace black top that I knew set off my auburn hair. Looking good would give me the confidence I needed to carry this through—I hoped.

As I drove up the winding driveway to his place, I looked out for Dave. Jeez, I hoped he was as friendly as Zach said he was. I saw the ute parked out the front, so at least Zach was home, though at this point I wasn't sure if I was relieved or not about that.

As I walked up to the front door, I heard Dave's deep chested barks from around the back. I looked warily around, but there was no sign of him hurtling towards me. I realised that he must be fenced in. Giving a relieved sigh,

I lifted my hand to knock at the front door, but before I had a chance, it was opened.

Zach looked down at me, surprised and waiting.

'Hi,' I said, 'Mind if I come in?'

# Chapter Fourteen

He opened the door wide and motioned for me to enter, then led the way to the lounge. I sat down on the sofa and he sat in the armchair opposite me. 'What's the problem?' He said. Both his tone and expression were guarded.

Of course he would think there was a problem. That seemed to be the only time I contacted him. I took a deep breath. 'No problem. I just have a few things to say to you.'

'Shoot,' he said. Not exactly a promising beginning. I might have been one of those door-to-door people trying to sell Foxtel or phone plans, for all the encouragement he was giving me.

I took a deep breath. 'I came to say thank you for taking me home on Sunday night. I wasn't in any condition to say it at the time, but I really appreciate it, and so does my sister.'

'No worries,' he said. 'You could have texted me. No need to come all the way out here for that.'

He wasn't making this easy for me. *Never mind, press on*, I told myself. 'I also wanted to say I was sorry. I've been an idiot. No one knows that better than me, and I haven't treated you very well at all. I judged you before I even knew you, and because of my stupid obsession with anything French, I never even gave you a chance. I really regret that.'

Did I see a softening of his expression? I continued, 'I think my main reason for asking André to dance was because I wanted to make you jealous.'

He looked at me in a considering way. 'Why did you want to make me jealous?'

It was time for the truth. 'Because that was how I felt when I saw you with Chelsea. I couldn't stand the way she was clinging on to you or the way you were holding her.'

'Why should you care? You've had your sights set on André LeBlanc for months. And now you know the truth about him, you're ready to settle for me?'

Perhaps I deserved that, but it still hurt. I turned my head to one side so he wouldn't see the tears that moistened my eyes. 'André never made me feel one tenth the way I did when I was with you,' I said softly.

The silence between us was heavy for a few moments before Zach spoke. 'I guess I have an apology to make, too. I should have told you who I was from the beginning. I wasn't completely honest. I was going to explain that night at Bart's. I brought Chelsea home and came back to see if I could talk to you. But, after what happened, I realised you really weren't interested in me.'

I wanted to tell him how wrong he was, but first, I wanted to hear what else he had to say. 'Charlotte said something about your family business,' I said. 'I was surprised you hadn't mentioned it before.'

'My sister,' he said, lifting his brows, 'She means well, but she has a big mouth.'

'Sisters. Tell me about them. But why weren't you upfront with me from the beginning?'

Zach gave a heavy sigh. 'It's hard to know where to start. But I guess I should plunge in and say what I do for a living. Charlotte and I jointly manage the chain stores, Isolde Interiors. You may have heard of them?'

*That was like saying you may have heard of Target or Woolies,* I thought, but said nothing. I waited for him to continue.

'I have a low-key lifestyle and I try to be as normal as possible. I don't go around broadcasting the fact that I've had a few more privileges than most people. Even when Mum and Dad were alive, they kept us grounded. Yes, we lived in a nice house, but they sent us to state schools, and we had to work for pocket money and everything. When they died, I didn't want to stay in their house, so we mainly use it for offices now. I bought this place where I could be myself, have Dave and try to fit into the neighbourhood.'

I nodded. It made sense the way he was telling it. I just wished he had told me earlier.

Zach continued, 'When I met you, that first time I saw you in French class, and you turned me down flat, I have to admit, I was surprised.'

I smiled. 'Your ego was dented, admit it.'

'It was good for me, though I didn't think so at the time. Then you became a challenge.'

'Oh, nice. I thought you were attracted to me.'

'I was, right from the moment I saw your red hair and those ridiculous high heels you were wearing.'

'Auburn, thanks, and those high heels cost half a week's salary.'

'Anyway, I couldn't believe my luck when your car wouldn't start. I was determined to make you interested, but I wanted to do it on my own, and not because I was some rich guy who wowed you.'

'So, you thought I was the type of girl who would be impressed by money and prestige?' I wasn't sure I liked the sound of that, but I realised that I might have deserved it.

'No, not exactly, but you seemed to judge me instantly, and made it clear you weren't interested in my kind of bloke. I wanted to change your mind about that, but I wanted you to like me for who I was and not what I was.'

His words made me realise just how prejudiced I had been. I had jumped to conclusions and they had been all the wrong ones. Thinking about that made me feel ashamed. I really had no right to blame Zach for not opening up to me, when I had given myself no opportunities to find out who he was as a person.

'I'm sorry, Zach. I wasn't very nice to you and I just gave you a lot of attitude.'

'You certainly kept me on my toes.'

'But, you know, I was attracted to you from the start, too. I just wouldn't admit it to myself. I had this stupid obsession about André, just because he was French. I never really knew him and to be honest, I never really felt anything for him. If I'd really looked at him as a person, I might have realised sooner that he was gay.'

'So,' Zach said, tilting his head and looking at me, 'You were attracted to me from the beginning, eh?'

I recognised that teasing tone. 'I might have been.' I gave him a look of my own.

'How are you feeling right now?'

'What do you think? I'm here, aren't I?'

'Yeah, but actions speak louder than words. So, what are you going to do about it?'

'What do you want me to do about it?'

He sat back in his armchair and patted his lap. 'You know this chair can easily hold two people. Want to test it out?'

I smiled. He wanted me to come to him for a change. I could do that. I got up and went over to him, and he pulled me into his arms. 'That's much better,' he said as he bent his face towards mine. 'I think we've got some serious catching up to do.'

'I quite agree,' I said. As his firm lips pressed against mine, I felt the heat spiral from the pit of my stomach. Wrapping my arms around his neck, I moulded my body to his. He gave a small groan as his hands travelled down my back, pressing me even closer so that I was in no doubt. Zach Mills wanted me and I sure as hell wanted him. Finally, we were in sync. Things I knew, hoped, could get very hot, very fast.

Just when things were getting interesting, the door was shoved open and the click of nails sounded on the floor. Before I had time to move, *whoosh*, a huge, furry canine jumped on top of us, and I felt long, slobbery licks on my face. The footrest of the lazy boy chair sprung out, sending the three of us backwards with a jerk. It was a small miracle it didn't break altogether, or that we didn't fall out.

'Dave, get down, you idiot,' Zach shouted.

But Dave was beside himself with joy, his tail thumping and his head, now he'd covered me in doggy kisses, resting on my shoulder.

Zach gave him a shove and he landed on the floor. I hopped off Zach, before Dave decided he'd relaunch himself at us. Zach got up and grabbed him by the collar. 'Outside, now. How you got in, I'll never know.'

I burst into laughter. After a moment, Zach shook his head and gave a chuckle. Dave, thinking he was enormously popular, gave an enthusiastic bark.

'Are you sure your family wants you to have a girlfriend? First Charlotte and now Dave? Their timing is perfect,' I said when my giggles had subsided.

'Are you kidding? Charlotte's your biggest fan, and you've just been welcomed officially into the family by Dave. But now, he's definitely going out. Come on, boy.'

As Dave was dragged away, he gave me a mournful look. I was almost tempted to ask Zach to let him stay. Almost, but not quite. I figured Zach and I had finally earned some alone time.

Zach took Dave outside and I sat on the sofa, not willing to take any more chances with that chair.

Much, much later, when we were curled up with a glass of wine, Zach said, 'I could get used to this. How about you?'

What? Was he still in doubt about my feelings, which I thought I'd made perfectly clear in the last little while?

'Zach, I like you. A lot. I'd like to get to know you much better, the real you. I think that's a pretty good start. And, yes, I could definitely get used to this.'

Putting his arm around me, he pulled me a little closer and rested his chin on top of my head.

'Then I guess I'd better be *totally* honest with you. One of the reasons I never told you I was part French, was because I was worried that might be the only reason you liked me.'

'You're what?' I sat up straight and looked at him.

'You never did ask me why I was studying French, did you? My mother was French Canadian, although we never spoke French at home. Charlotte and I still have grandparents living in Quebec. She's been over several times to visit them, but I haven't been since I was a kid. I'm planning to go over at Christmas to see them, so I was brushing up on my French for that reason.'

It was one of the few times in my life that I was absolutely speechless.

He pulled me back in close to his side and grinned down at me. 'Come on, don't you think that makes me sexier now?'

I wasn't going to let him off the hook that easily, after dropping a bombshell like that. 'You know, I've gone off all things French. I threw out my French posters and my guidebook, and I haven't gone back to French class.'

'You've already told me you like me. Too late to go back on that now.'

A sudden thought hit me. 'You haven't actually said you like me, though. You've said you were attracted, interested—blah, blah blah—but not that you really like me, the real, flawed and accident prone me.'

He laughed and said, 'That's the part I like the most about you, because it brought us together so often. Then he lowered his head and said softly, 'But, I'll do more than just tell you, let me show you, *chérie.*'

'I agree. There's been enough talking, for now.' Then, I showed Zach Mills just how sexy I found him, French or not.

# Epilogue

**Christmas - eight months later**

I was going to Quebec. That was a definite. With my ticket purchased—with some careful budgeting from my part-time job—there was no question over when. I had visualised it, looked at guidebooks with Zach, put Canadian posters up of Quebec City and Montreal, and practised making pancakes with real maple syrup. I'd even started a Bachelor of Education course, with a major in French. Really, except for the fine print, I was there.

And, my boyfriend. Zach Mills. Sigh. He was not your typical Aussie or even French bloke. But I wouldn't have him any other way. How he ended up in Clearwater Creek, I don't know. Unless it was to meet me. There you go, the law of attraction. I wished for someone fantastic, thought it and—voilà, Zach Mills appeared in my French class.

Don't tell me the power of positive thinking doesn't work.

# Acknowledgements

Any book, short or long, is always due to the efforts of more than just the author, and this one is no exception. Originally published in 2013, *Bonjour Cherie* has undergone editing and updating, thanks to feedback from several people, especially my daughter, Ruth, who has really helped me to make this book more timely and relevant. Thanks also to my writer friends in the Rainforest Writers' Retreat and Write Links, whose insights and suggestions have helped my writing move to the next level. And, of course, where would I be without my readers? I am so grateful for their support and feedback. Finally, a big shout out to Anthony and the team at the Self Publishing Lab, who have done it again with their amazing production and cover.

# To my readers

I hope you enjoyed *Bonjour Cherie,* the second novella in *Short Sweetz,* a collection of stand alone books, full of heart and humour. They are the perfect escape for an hour or two whether you're having a coffee, catching the train, or just want to chill. If you have the time, I would love it if you could leave a review of the book on your favourite retail site.

# About the author

**Robin Martin** is an author and teacher, who writes both adult and young adult romance. Originally from Canada, she now lives just outside Brisbane, Australia. Writing has always been her passion, and in recent years she has written several novels for young adults and adults, including *The Alien Chronicles*, and the *Short Sweetz* series.

When she is not plotting stories, she loves reading everything from cereal boxes to long novels she can get lost in. Robin finds her inspiration in long walks along the beautiful Queensland coast, listening to an eclectic music collection that ranges from the Rolling Stones to Mozart, and good coffee, without which she wouldn't be able to function.

She is a member of *Write Links* and the *Rainforest Writers' Retreat*. Visit Robin at www.robinmartinthomas.com to find out about all her books, and to sign up for her newsletter to receive free stories and the latest updates on her next books. You can also check out her author Facebook page at https://www.facebook.com/robinmartinthomas or follow her on Instagram @georgi_two_martini